THE

C000057412

NORA ROBERTS

THE *Gift*

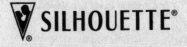

SILHOUETTE®

DID YOU PURCHASE THIS BOOK WITHOUT A COVER?
If you did, you should be aware it is **stolen property** as it was
reported *unsold and destroyed* by a retailer. Neither the author nor
the publisher has received any payment for this book.

*All the characters in this book have no existence outside the
imagination of the author, and have no relation whatsoever to anyone
bearing the same name or names. They are not even distantly inspired
by any individual known or unknown to the author, and all the
incidents are pure invention.*

*All Rights Reserved including the right of reproduction in whole or
in part in any form. This edition is published by arrangement with
Harlequin Enterprises II B.V. The text of this publication or any part
thereof may not be reproduced or transmitted in any form or by any
means, electronic or mechanical, including photocopying, recording,
storage in an information retrieval system, or otherwise, without the
written permission of the publisher.*

*This book is sold subject to the condition that it shall not, by way of
trade or otherwise, be lent, resold, hired out or otherwise circulated
without the prior consent of the publisher in any form of binding or
cover other than that in which it is published and without a similar
condition including this condition being imposed on the subsequent
purchaser.*

*Silhouette and Colophon are registered trademarks of
Harlequin Books S.A., used under licence.*

*Silhouette Books, Eton House, 18-24 Paradise Road,
Richmond, Surrey TW9 1SR*

THE GIFT © Harlequin Books S.A. 2004

The publisher acknowledges the copyright holder of the
individual works as follows:

Home for Christmas © Nora Roberts 1986
All I Want for Christmas © Nora Roberts 1994

ISBN-13: 978 0 263 85543 2
ISBN-10: 0 263 85543 0

059-1206

*Printed and bound in Spain
by Litografia Rosés S.A., Barcelona*

CONTENTS

HOME FOR CHRISTMAS 13

ALL I WANT FOR CHRISTMAS 147

Dear Reader,

Silhouette Books is proud to present a rare treat for the holidays. *The Gift* features two heartwarming tales of holiday love and family from the master of romance, Nora Roberts. Previously offered in our popular Silhouette Christmas collections, these stories have been unavailable to readers for over a decade—until now.

In "Home for Christmas," a reporter who's wandered the globe for years returns home, determined to win back the heart of the woman he left behind. But she has responsibilities that cannot be tossed aside—even for the man she'd never stopped loving. Will this Christmas together lead to a lifetime of comfort and joy?

No one can resist twins, not even Santa! That's what identical brothers Zeke and Zack are hoping when they ask jolly St Nick for a new mum. They're sure their new music teacher's the perfect addition to their family. Now they have to convince their dad! Will the magic of Christmas wishes come true for two adorable boys, in "All I Want for Christmas"?

And as an extra-special bonus, take a look at our mini holiday cookbook, with three of Nora's holiday recipes, with personal notes from the author herself. We hope you and your family enjoy these tasty treats!

May all your Christmas wishes come true this holiday season!

Happy holiday!

The Editors
Silhouette Books

NORA ROBERTS'S
HOLIDAY RECIPES

POP'S PANCAKES

A long-time tradition in my family is Christmas breakfast. My parents' home was always crowded and noisy, and everyone lent a hand—watching the light on the waffle iron, holding their plates out for more. We were allowed to fry the bacon or flip the pancakes on the griddle. But nobody—nobody—made the pancake batter except my pop. There were two huge bowls of it to feed the horde before we got down to exchanging gifts and ripping coloured paper to shreds. Because there were so many of us, we often ate in shifts, crowding around the dining room table and spilling over to the breakfast bar. Wherever I sit, the first bite takes me back to childhood.

6 eggs, beaten
1 can evaporated milk
60g butter or margarine, melted
12fl oz regular milk (8fl oz for waffles)
750g flour
6 tbsp baking powder

Combine ingredients in the order listed. Mix well. Let stand for 10 minutes to rise. For pancakes, spoon batter onto hot griddle. Be patient—don't flip until bubbles appear.
Enjoy!

PLAIN OR PAINTED HOLIDAY COOKIES

Baking helps put me in the mood for the holidays. There's nothing like a little flour on your hands to start "Jingle Bells" ringing in your head. The tradition in my house goes this way: first put on an album of Christmas music. It isn't possible to work over a hot oven without the proper setting. Gather your ingredients:

6fl oz shortening (butter or margarine could substitute)
250g sugar
2 eggs
1 tsp vanilla extract
625g flour
1 tsp baking powder
1 tsp salt
Optional: evaporated milk, food colouring, small
paintbrush, coloured sugar or sprinkles

If you have kids, this is the time to step back and let them do some of the work. It makes it fun, and the mess is almost worth it. Let one of them mix the shortening and sugar together. Let another one crack the eggs into the bowl. Then you can help by picking out the pieces of eggshell. Add the vanilla extract and mix thoroughly. Blend in flour, baking powder and salt. Cover and chill for at least an hour.

Preheat your oven to 200°C/gas mark 6. Now comes the time when the kids fight over who rolls out the dough. See that it's rolled about an 1/8" thick on a floured board. If you don't have cookie cutters in cute little Christmas shapes, you should. We generally stick to the tried-and-true angels, Santas and trees.

When you cut the cookies, make sure to dip the cutter into flour now and then or you'll end up with a jammed-up Santa. Place cookies on an ungreased baking sheet. Now you can either sprinkle them with plain or coloured sugar and be done with them, or if you're feeling adventurous you can use that little paintbrush. Divide small amounts of evaporated milk into several cups, along with a little food colouring in each. Then go ahead and paint. Remember, it doesn't matter if Santa's blue or the Christmas tree is red. And just add a little water as the mixture thickens.

Bake for six or seven minutes. Break off a couple of times to sing a round of "Deck the Halls." You'll feel better. You should have about four dozen cookies, but then, if you have children, forget it. When your husband comes home and asks what's for dinner, shove a cookie in his mouth!

OLD-FASHIONED BREAD PUDDING

I do a lot of complicated baking at this time of year—time-consuming treats that keep me in the kitchen for hours. I really don't mind, but there's something to be said for simplicity. One of my men's favourites is an old family recipe handed down through the Scottish branch of my family, through my father to me. It's wonderfully simple and old-fashioned, something that can literally be tossed together when you discover unexpected holiday visitors are coming to call. Best of all, since it's made in one dish, there's little to clean up. I should warn you, most of the measurements are estimates. Experiment. It's that kind of dish.

6 to 8 slices bread, torn into pieces
3 to 4 eggs, lightly beaten
60g margarine, melted
60-80g sugar
24-28 fl oz milk
About 60g raisins (it's up to you)
Cinnamon to taste (I like a lot myself, maybe 3 tbsp or so. I really don't measure—I go by how it looks.)

Preheat oven to 200°C/gas mark 6. Mix all ingredients, gently but thoroughly, in a casserole dish. Pop it into the oven for 1 hour. Can be eaten warm or cold.

HOME FOR CHRISTMAS

Chapter 1

So much can change in ten years. He was prepared for it. All during the flight from London and the long, winding drive north from Boston to Quiet Valley, New Hampshire, population 326—or it had been ten years before when Jason Law had last been there—he'd thought of how different things would be. A decade, even for a forgotten little town in New England was bound to bring changes. There would have been deaths and births. Houses and shops would have changed hands. Some of them might not be there at all.

Not for the first time since Jason had de-

cided to visit his hometown did he feel foolish.
After all, it was very likely he wouldn't even
be recognized. He'd left a thin, defiant twenty-
year-old in a scruffy pair of jeans. He was
coming back a man who'd learned how to replace defiance with arrogance and succeed.
His frame was still lean, but it fitted nicely into
clothes tailored on Savile Row and Seventh
Avenue. Ten years had changed him from a
desperate boy determined to make his mark to
an outwardly complacent man who had. What
ten years hadn't changed, was what was inside. He was still looking for roots, for his
place. That was why he was heading back to
Quiet Valley.

The road still twisted and turned through
the woods, up the mountains and down again,
as it had when he'd headed in the opposite
direction on a Greyhound. Snow covered the
ground, smooth here, bumpy there where it
was heaped over rocks. In the sunlight trees
shimmered with it. Had he missed it? He'd
spent one winter in snow up to his waist in
the Andes. He'd spent another sweltering in
Africa. The years ran together, but oddly

enough, Jason could remember every place he'd spent Christmas over the last ten years, though he'd never celebrated the holiday. The road narrowed and swept into a wide curve. He could see the mountains, covered with pines and dusted with white. Yes, he'd missed it.

Sun bounced off the mounds of snow. He adjusted his dark glasses and slowed down, then on impulse, stopped. When he stepped from the car his breath came in streams of smoke. His skin tingled with the cold but he didn't button his coat or reach in his pockets for his gloves. He needed to feel it. Breathing in the thin, icy air was like breathing in thousands of tiny needles. Jason walked the few feet to the top of the ridge and looked down on Quiet Valley.

He'd been born there, raised there. He'd learned of grief there—and he'd fallen in love. Even from the distance he could see her house—her parents' house, Jason reminded himself and felt the old, familiar surge of fury. She'd be living somewhere else now, with her husband, with her children.

When he discovered that his hands were balled into fists he carefully relaxed them. Channeling emotion was a skill he'd turned into an art over the past decade. If he could do it in his work, reporting on famine, war, and suffering, he could do it for himself. His feelings for Faith had been a boy's feelings. He was a man now, and she, like Quiet Valley, was only part of his childhood. He'd traveled more than five thousand miles just to prove it. Turning away, he got back in the car and started down the mountain.

From the distance, Quiet Valley had looked like a Currier and Ives painting, all white and snug between mountain and forest. As he drew closer, it became less idyllic and more approachable. The tired paint showed here and there on some of the outlying houses. Fences bowed under snow. He saw a few new houses in what had once been open fields. Change. He reminded himself he'd expected it.

Smoke puffed out of chimneys. Dogs and children raced in the snow. A check of his watch showed him it was half past three. School was out, and he'd been traveling for fifteen hours. The smart thing to do was to see if the Valley Inn was still in operation and get a room. A smile played around his mouth as he wondered if old Mr. Beantree still ran the place. He couldn't count the times Beantree had told him he'd never amount to anything but trouble. He had a Pulitzer and an Overseas Press Award to prove differently.

Houses were grouped closer together now, and he recognized them. The Bedford place, Tim Hawkin's house, the Widow Marchant's. He slowed again as he passed the widow's tidy blue clapboard. She hadn't changed the color, he noticed and felt foolishly pleased. And the old spruce in the front yard was already covered with bright-red ribbons. She'd been kind to him. Jason hadn't forgotten how she had fixed hot chocolate and listened to him for hours when he'd told her of the travels he wanted to make, the places he dreamed of seeing. She'd been in her seventies when he'd left, but of tough New England stock. He thought he might still find her in her kitchen patiently fueling the wood stove and listening to her Rachmaninoff.

The streets of the town were clear and tidy. New Englanders were a practical lot, and Jason thought, as sturdy as the bedrock they'd planted themselves on. The town had not changed as he'd anticipated. Railings Hardware still sat on the corner off Main and the post office still occupied a brick building no bigger than a garage. The same red garland was strung from lamppost to lamppost as it had been all through his youth during each holiday season. Children were building a snowman in front of the Litner place. But whose children? Jason wondered. He scanned the red mufflers and bright boots knowing any of them might be Faith's. The fury came back and he looked away.

The sign on the Valley Inn had been repainted, but nothing else about the three-story square stone building was different. The walkway had been scraped clean and smoke billowed out of both chimneys. He found himself driving beyond it. There was something else to do first, something he'd already known he would have to do. He could have turned at the corner, driven a block and seen the house where he grew up. But he didn't.

Near the end of Main would be a tidy white house, bigger than most of the others with two big bay windows and a wide front porch. Tom Monroe had brought his bride there. A reporter of Jason's caliber knew how to ferret out such information. Perhaps Faith had put up the lace curtains she'd always wanted at the windows. Tom would have bought her the pretty china tea sets she'd longed for. He'd have given her exactly what she'd wanted. Jason would have given her a suitcase and a motel room in countless cities. She'd made her choice.

After ten years he discovered it was no easier to accept. Still, he forced himself to be calm as he pulled up to the curb. He and Faith had been friends once, lovers briefly. He'd had other lovers since, and she had a husband. But he could still remember her as she'd looked at eighteen, lovely, soft, eager. She had wanted to go with him, but he wouldn't let her. She had promised to wait, but she hadn't. He took a deep breath as he climbed from the car.

The house was lovely. In the big bay window that faced the street was a Christmas tree, cluttered and green in the daylight. At night it would glitter like magic. He could be sure of it because Faith had always believed so strongly in magic.

Standing on the sidewalk he found himself dealing with fear. He'd covered wars and interviewed terrorists but he'd never felt the stomach-churning fear that he did now, standing on a narrow snow-brushed sidewalk facing a pristine white house with holly bushes by the door. He could turn around, he reminded himself. Drive back to the inn or simply out of town again. There was no need to see her again. She was out of his life. Then he saw the lace curtains at the window and the old resentment stirred, every bit as strong as fear.

As he started down the walk a girl raced around the side of the house just ahead of a well-aimed snowball. She dived, rolled and evaded. In an instant, she was up again and hurling one of her own.

"Bull's-eye, Jimmy Harding!" With a whoop, she turned to run and barreled into Jason. "Sorry." With snow covering her from head to foot, she looked up and grinned. Jason felt the world spin backward.

She was the image of her mother. The sable hair peeked out of her cap and fell untidily to her shoulders. The small, triangular face was dominated by big blue eyes that seemed to hold jokes all of their own. But it was the smile, the one that said, isn't this fun? that caught him by the throat. Shaken, he stepped back while the girl dusted herself off and studied him.

"I've never seen you before."

He slipped his hands into his pockets. But I've seen you, he thought. "No. Do you live here?"

"Yeah, but the shop's around the side." A snowball landed with a plop at her feet. She lifted a brow in a sophisticated manner. "That's Jimmy," she said in the tone of a woman barely tolerating a suitor. "His aim's lousy. The shop's around the side," she repeated as she bent to ball more snow. "Just walk right in."

She raced off holding a ball in each hand. Jason figured Jimmy was in for a surprise.

Faith's daughter. He hadn't asked her name and nearly called her back. It didn't matter, he told himself. He'd only be in town a few days before he took the next assignment. Just passing through, he thought. Just cleaning the slate.

He backtracked to walk around the side of the house. Though he couldn't imagine what sort of shop Tom could have, he thought it might be best to see him first. He almost relished it.

The little workshop he'd half expected turned out to be a miniature of a Victorian cottage. The sleigh out in front held two life-size dolls dressed in top hats and bonnets, cloaks and top boots. Above the door was a fancy hand-painted sign that read Doll House. To the accompaniment of bells, Jason pushed the door open.

"I'll be right with you."

Hearing her voice again was like stepping back and finding no solid ground. But he'd deal with it, Jason told himself. He'd deal with it because he had to. Slipping off his glasses, he tucked them into his pocket and looked around.

Child-size furniture was set around the room in the manner of a cozy parlor. Dolls of every shape and size and style occupied chairs, stools, shelves and cabinets. In front of an elf-size fireplace where flames shimmered, sat a grandmother of a doll in lace cap and apron. The illusion was so strong Jason almost expected her to begin rocking.

"I'm sorry to keep you waiting." With a china doll in one hand and a bridal veil in the other, Faith walked through the doorway. "I was right in the middle of..." The veil floated out of her hand as she stopped. It waltzed to the floor with no sound at all. Color rushed away from her face, making the deep-blue eyes nearly violet in contrast. In reaction, or defense, she gripped the doll to her breast. "Jason."

Chapter 2

Framed in the doorway with the thin winter light creeping through the tiny windows she was lovelier than his memory of her. He'd hoped it would be different. He'd hoped his fantasies of her would be exaggerated as so many fantasies are. But she was here, flesh and blood, and so beautiful she took his breath away. Perhaps because of it, his smile was cynical and his voice cool.

"Hello, Faith."

She couldn't move, forward or back. He trapped her now as he had so many years before. He didn't know it then, she couldn't let

him know it now. Emotion, locked and kept
secret for so long struggled against will and
was held back. "How are you?" she managed
to ask, her hands like a vise around the doll.

"Fine." He walked toward her. God, how
it pleased him to see the nerves jumping in her
eyes. God, how it tormented him to learn she
smelled the same. Soft, young, innocent. "You
look wonderful." He said it carelessly, like a
yawn.

"You were the last person I expected to see
walk through the door." One she'd learned to
stop looking for. Determined to control herself, Faith loosened her grip on the doll. "How
long are you in town?"

"Just a few days. I had the urge."

She laughed and hoped it didn't sound hys-
terical. "You always did. We read a lot about
you. You've been able to see all the places you
always wanted to see."

"And more."

She turned away, giving herself a moment
to close her eyes and pull her emotions together. "They ran it on the front page when
you won the Pulitzer. Mr. Beantree strutted

around as though he'd been your mentor. 'Fine boy, Jason Law,' he said. 'Always knew he'd amount to something.'"

"I saw your daughter."

That was the biggest fear, the biggest hope, the dream she'd put to rest years ago. She bent casually to pick up the veil. "Clara?"

"Just outside. She was about to mow down some boy named Jimmy."

"Yes, that's Clara." The smile came quickly and just as stunningly as it had on the child. "She's a vicious competitor," she added and wanted to say like her father, but didn't dare.

There was so much to say, so much that couldn't be said. If he had had one wish at that moment it would have been to reach out and touch her. Just to touch her once and remember the way it had been.

"I see you have your lace curtains."

Regret washed over her. She'd have settled for bare windows, blank walls. "Yes, I have my lace curtains and you your adventures."

"And this place." He turned to look around again. "When did all this start?"

She could deal with it, she promised herself,

this hatefully casual small talk. "I opened it nearly eight years ago now."

He picked a rag doll from a bassinet. "So you sell dolls. A hobby?"

Something else came into her eyes now. Strength. "No, it's my business. I sell them, repair them, even make them."

"Business?" He set the doll down and the smile he gave her had nothing to do with humor. "It's hard for me to picture Tom approving of his wife setting up a business."

"Is it?" It hurt, but she set the china doll on a counter and began to arrange the veil on its head. "You always were perceptive, Jason, but you've been away a long time." She looked over her shoulder and her eyes weren't nervous or even strong. They were simply cold. "A very long time. Tom and I were divorced eight years ago. The last time I heard he was living in Los Angeles. You see, he didn't care for small towns either. Or small-town girls."

He couldn't name the things that stirred in him so he pushed them aside. Bitterness was simpler. "Apparently you picked badly, Faith."

She laughed again but the veil crumpled in her hand. "Apparently I did."

"You didn't wait." It was out before he could stop it. He hated himself for it, and her.

"You were gone." She turned back slowly and folded her hands.

"I told you I'd come back. I told you I'd send for you as soon as I could."

"You never called, or wrote. For three months I—"

"Three months?" Furious, he grabbed her arms. "After everything we'd talked about, everything we'd hoped for, three months was all you could give me?"

She would have given him a lifetime, but there hadn't been a choice. Struggling to keep her voice calm, she looked into his eyes. They were the same—intense, impatient. "I didn't know where you were. You wouldn't even give me that." She pulled away from him because the need was as great as it had always been. "I was eighteen and you were gone."

"And Tom was here."

She set her jaw. "And Tom was here. It's been ten years, Jason, you never once wrote. Why now?"

"I've asked myself the same thing," he murmured and left her standing alone.

Her dreams had always been too fanciful. As a child Faith had envisioned white chargers and glass slippers. Reality was something to be faced daily in a family where money was scarce and pride was not, but dreams weren't just for nighttime.

She'd fallen in love with Jason when she'd been eight and he ten and he'd bravely vanquished three boys who'd tossed her into the snow. It had taken three of them. Faith could still look back on that with a sense of satisfaction. But it had been Jason fiercely coming to her rescue and sending her opponents scattering that she remembered best. He'd been thin, and his coat had been too large and mended at the elbows. She remembered his eyes, deep, deep brown under brows drawn close in annoyance as he'd looked down at her. Snow had coated his pale-blond hair and reddened his face. She'd looked into his eyes and fallen in love. He'd muttered at her, hauled her up and scolded her for getting in

trouble. Then he'd stalked off with his un-
gloved hands thrust into the pockets of his
too-big coat.

Through childhood and into adolescence
she'd never looked at another boy. Of course
she'd pretended to from time to time hoping
it might make Jason Law notice her.

Then when she'd been sixteen and her
mother had sewn her a dress for the spring
dance at the town hall, he'd noticed. So had
several other boys, and Faith had flirted outrageously, with one goal in mind: Jason Law.
Sulky and defiant he'd watched her dance with
one boy after another. She'd made sure of it.
Just as she'd made sure she looked directly at
him before she'd stepped outside to take the
air. He'd followed her, just as she'd hoped.
She'd pretended to be sophisticated. He'd been
rude. And he'd walked her home under a fat
full moon.

There'd been other walks after that—
spring, summer, fall, winter. They were in love
as only the young can be, carelessly, heedlessly, innocently. She told him of her longings
for a house and children, for lace curtains and

china cups. He told her of his passion to travel, to see everything, and write it down. She knew he'd felt trapped in the small town, hampered by a father who gave him no love and little hope. He knew she dreamed of quiet rooms with flowers in crystal vases. But they were drawn together and tangled all the dreams into one.

Then one night in the summer when the air was sweet with wild grass they stopped being children and their love stopped being innocent.

"Mom, you're dreaming again."

"What?" Up to her elbows in soapy water, Faith turned. Her daughter stood at the doorway to the kitchen, snugly wrapped in a flannel gown that came up to her chin. With her hair freshly brushed and her face scrubbed clean, she looked like an angel. Faith knew better. "I guess I was. You've finished your homework?"

"Yeah. It's dumb having homework when school's nearly out."

"Don't remind me."

"You're grumpy," Clara declared and eyed

the cookie jar. "You should go for one of your walks."

"Just one," Faith said, easily outguessing her daughter. "And don't forget to brush your teeth." She waited while Clara rooted through the jar. "Did you see a man this afternoon? A tall man with blond hair?"

"Uh-huh." Mouth full, Clara turned back to her mother. "He was walking up to the house. I sent him to the shop."

"Did he—say anything to you?"

"Not really. He looked at me kind of funny at first, like he'd seen me before. Do you know him?"

While her heart began a slow, dull thud, Faith dried her hands. "Yes. He used to live here a long time ago."

"Oh. Jimmy liked his car." She wondered if she could talk herself into another cookie.

"I think I will take that walk, Clara, but I want you in bed."

Recognizing the tone, she knew the cookie would have to wait. "Can I count the presents under the tree again?"

"You've counted them ten times."

"Maybe there's a new one."

Laughing, Faith gathered her up. "Not a chance." Then she grinned and carried Clara into the living room. "But it won't hurt to count them one more time."

The air was brittle when she stepped outside and it smelled of snow. There was no reason to lock the doors in a town where she knew everyone. Bundling her coat closer, she glanced back at the second-story window where her daughter slept. Clara was the reason why the house wasn't cold, why her life wasn't empty when both things could easily have been true.

She'd left the tree burning and the lights around the door sent out festive color. Four days until Christmas, she thought, and the wonder of it came home again. From where she stood, the town looked as pretty as a postcard with the strings of lights, the tree with its star in the town square, the street lamps burning. She could smell smoke from the chimneys and the bursting scent of pine.

Some might find it too settled, others would find it dull. But Faith had made it a home for herself and her daughter. She'd altered her life to suit her, and it fitted her well.

No regrets, she promised with one last glance at her daughter's window. No regrets at all.

The wind picked up a bit as she walked. There'd be snow for Christmas. She could feel it. She'd look forward to that, not back any longer.

"Still fond of walking?"

Chapter 3

Had she known he'd find her? Perhaps she had. Perhaps she'd needed him to. "Some things don't change," she said simply as Jason fell into step beside her.

"I've found that out in one afternoon." He thought of the town that had stayed so much the same. And of his feelings for the woman beside him. "Where's your daughter?"

"She's sleeping."

He was calmer than he'd been that afternoon, and determined to stay that way. "I didn't ask you if you had other children."

"No." He heard the wistfulness in her voice, just a sigh of it. "There's only Clara."

"How did you pick the name?"

She smiled. It was so like him to ask questions no one else would think of. "From the Nutcracker. I wanted her to be able to dream." As she had. Dropping her hands in her pockets she told herself they were simply two old friends walking through a quiet town. "Are you staying at the inn?"

"Yeah." Amused, Jason rubbed a hand over his chin. "Beantree took my bags up himself."

"Local boy makes good." She turned to look at him. It was easier somehow walking like this. Odd, she realized, she'd seen the boy when she'd looked at him the first time. Now she saw the man. His hair had darkened a bit but was still very blond. It was no longer unkempt, but cut in a carelessly attractive style that had it falling over his brow. His face was still thin, hollow at the cheeks in the way that had always fascinated her. And his mouth was still full, but there was a hardness around it that hadn't been there once. "You did make good, didn't you? You made everything you wanted happen."

"Most everything." When his eyes met hers

she felt all the old longings come back. "What about you, Faith?"

She shook her head, watching the sky as she walked. "I never wanted as much as you, Jason."

"Are you happy?"

"If a person isn't, it's their own fault."

"That's too simple."

"I haven't seen the things you've seen. I haven't had to deal with what you've had to deal with. I am simple, Jason. That was the problem, wasn't it?"

"No." He turned her to face him and slid his hands up to her face. He wore no gloves, and his fingers warmed against her skin. "God, you haven't changed." As she stood very still he combed his fingers up through her hair, then down to where the tips brushed her shoulders. "I've thought about the way you look in the moonlight countless times. It was just like this."

"I've changed, Jason." But her voice was breathless. "So have you."

"Some things don't," he reminded her and gave in to the need.

When his mouth touched hers, he knew that he'd come home. Everything he remembered, everything he thought he'd lost was his again. She was soft and smelled of springtime even when snow dusted the ground around them. Her mouth was willing, even as it had been the first time he'd tasted it. He couldn't explain, even to himself, that every other woman he'd held had been nothing but a shadow of his memory of her. Now she was real, wrapped in his arms and giving him everything he'd forgotten he could have.

Just once, she promised herself as she melted against him. Just once more. How could she have known her life had such a void in it? She'd tried to close the door on the part of her life that included Jason, though she'd known it wasn't possible. She'd tried to tell herself it was only youthful passion and girlish fancy but she'd known that was a lie. There'd been no other men, only memories of one, and wishes, half-forgotten dreams.

She was holding no memory now but Jason, as real and urgent as he'd always been. Everything about him was so familiar, the taste of his lips on hers, the feel of his hair as her fingers raked through it, the scent of man, rough and rugged, that he'd always carried with him even as a boy. He murmured her name and drew her closer, as if the years were trying to separate them again.

She wrapped her arms around him, as willing, as eager, and as in love as she'd been the last time he'd held her. The wind whipped around their ankles, puffing up clouds of snow while the moonlight held them close.

But it wasn't yesterday, she reminded herself as she stepped back. It wasn't tomorrow. It was today, and today had to be faced. She wasn't a child any longer without responsibilities and a love so big it overshadowed anything else. She was a woman with a child to raise and a home to make. He was a gypsy. He'd never pretended to be anything else.

"It's over for us, Jason." But she held his hand a moment longer. "It's been over for a long time."

"No." He caught her before she could turn away. "It isn't. I told myself it was, and that I'd come back and prove it. You've been eating at me half my life, Faith. It's never going to be over."

"You left me." The tears she promised herself she wouldn't shed spilled over. "You broke my heart. It's barely had time to mend, Jason. You won't break it again."

"You know I had to leave. If you'd waited—"

"It doesn't matter now." With a shake of her head she backed away. She would never be able to explain to him why it hadn't been possible to wait. "It doesn't matter because in a few days you'll be gone again. I won't let you whirl in and out of my life and leave my emotions in chaos. We both made our choices, Jason."

"Damn it, I missed you."

She closed her eyes. When she opened them again they were dry. "I had to stop missing you. Please leave me alone, Jason. If I thought we could be friends—"

"We always were."

"Always is gone." Nonetheless she held out both hands and took his. "Oh, Jason, you were my best friend, but I can't welcome you home because you scare the hell out of me."

"Faith." He curled his fingers around hers. "We need more time, to talk."

Looking at him she let out a long breath. "You know where to find me, Jason. You always did."

"Let me walk you home."

"No." Calmer, she smiled. "Not this time."

From the window of his room, Jason could see most of Main Street. He could, if he chose, watch the flow of business in Porterfield's Five and Dime or the collection of people who walked through and loitered in the town square. Too often he found the direction of his gaze wandering to the white house near the end of the street. Because he'd been restless, Jason had been up and at the window when Faith had walked outside with Clara to see her off to school with a group of other children. He'd seen her crouch down to adjust the collar of her daughter's coat. And he'd seen her stand, hatless, her back to him, as she'd watched the children drag themselves off for a day of books. She'd stood there a long time with the wind pulling and tugging at her hair,

and he'd waited for her to turn, to look at the
inn, to acknowledge somehow that she knew
he was there. But she'd walked around the
side of the house to her shop without looking
back.

Now, hours later, he was at the window
again, still restless. From the number of people
he could see walk back to the Doll House, her
business was thriving. She was working, busy,
while he was standing unshaven at a window
with his portable typewriter sitting silent on
the desk beside him.

He'd planned to work on his novel for a few
days—the novel he'd promised himself he'd
write. It was just one more promise he'd never
been able to keep because of the demands of
travel and reporting. He'd expected to be able
to work here, in the quiet, settled town of his
youth away from the demands of journalism
and the fast pace he'd set for himself. He'd
expected a lot of things. What he hadn't expected was to find himself just as wildly in
love with Faith as he'd been at twenty.

Jason turned away from the window and
stared at his typewriter. The papers were

there, notes bulging in manila envelopes, the half-finished manuscript pages. He could sit down and make himself work through the day into the night. He had the discipline for it. But in his life there was more than a book that was half finished. He was just coming to realize it.

By the time he'd shaved and dressed, it was past noon. He thought briefly about walking across the street to Mindy's to see if she still served the best homemade soup in town. But he didn't feel like chatty counter talk. Deliberately he turned south, away from Faith. He wouldn't make a fool of himself by chasing after her.

As he walked, he passed a half a dozen people he knew. He was greeted with thumps on the back, handshakes and avid curiosity. He'd strolled down the Left Bank, up Carnaby Street and along the narrow streets of Venice. After a decade of absence he found the walk down Main Street just as fascinating. There was a barber pole that swirled up and around and back into itself. A life-size cardboard Santa stood outside a dress shop gesturing passersby inside.

Spotting a display of poinsettias, Jason slipped into the store and bought the biggest one he could carry. The saleswoman had been in his graduating class and detained him for ten minutes before he could escape. He'd expected questions, but he hadn't guessed that he'd become the town celebrity. Amused, he made his way down the street as he had countless times before. When he reached the Widow Marchant's, he didn't bother with the front door. Following an old habit, he went around the back and knocked on the storm door. It still rattled. It was a small thing that pleased him enormously.

When the widow opened the door, and her little bird's eyes peered through the bright-red leaves of the flowers, he found himself grinning like a ten-year-old.

"It's about time," she said as she let him in. "Wipe your feet."

"Yes, ma'am." Jason scrubbed his boots against the rough mat before he set down the poinsettia on her kitchen table.

No more than five feet tall, the widow stood with her hands on her hips. She was bent a bit

with age and her face was a melody of lines
and wrinkles. The bib apron she wore was
covered with flour. Jason smelled cookies in
the oven and heard the majestic sound of clas-
sical music from the living-room speakers. The
widow nodded at the flowers.

"You always went for the big statement."
When she turned to look him up and down,
Jason found himself automatically standing
tall. "Put on a few pounds I see, but more
wouldn't hurt. Come, give me a kiss."

He bent to peck her cheek dutifully, then
found himself gathering her close. She felt
frail; he hadn't realized it by looking at her,
but she still smelled of all the good things he
remembered—soap and powder and warm
sugar.

"You don't seem surprised to see me," he
murmured as he straightened up.

"I knew you were here." She turned to fuss
at the oven because her eyes had filled. "I
knew before the ink dried where you signed
the registration at the inn. Sit down and take
off your coat. I have to get these cookies out."

He sat quietly while she worked and absorbed the feeling of home. It was here he'd always been able to come as a child and feel safe. While he watched, she began to heat chocolate in a dented little pan on the stove.

"How long you staying?"

"I don't know. I'm supposed to be in Hong Kong in a couple of weeks."

"Hong Kong." The widow pursed her lips as she arranged cookies on a plate. "You've been to all your places, Jason. Were they as exciting as you thought?"

"Some were." He stretched out his legs. He'd forgotten what it was to relax, body, soul and mind. "Some weren't."

"Now you've come home." She walked over to put the cookies on the table. "Why?"

He could be evasive with anyone else. He could even lie to himself. But with her there could only be the truth. "Faith."

"It always was." Back at the stove, she stirred the chocolate. He'd been a troubled boy, now he was a troubled man. "You heard she married Tom."

And with her, he didn't have to hide the bitterness. "Six months after I left I called. I'd landed a job with *Today's News*. They were sending me to a hole in the wall in Chicago, but it was something. I called Faith, but I got her mother. She was very kind, even sympathetic when she told me that Faith was married, had been married for three months and was going to have a baby. I hung up, I got drunk. In the morning I went to Chicago." He plucked a cookie from the plate and shrugged. "Life goes on, right?"

"It does, whether it tows us along with it or rolls right over us. And now that you know she's divorced?"

"We promised each other something. She married someone else."

She made a sound like steam escaping from a kettle. "You're a man now from the looks of you, not a bull-headed boy. Faith Kirkpatrick—"

"Faith Monroe," he reminded her.

"All right then." Patiently, she poured heated chocolate into mugs. After she set them on the table, she seated herself with a quiet wheeze. "Faith is a strong, beautiful woman inside and out. She's raising that little girl all alone and doing a good job of it. She's started a business and she's making it work. Alone. I know something about being alone."

"If she'd waited—"

"Well, she didn't. Whatever thoughts I have about her reasons I'm keeping to myself."

"Why did she divorce Tom?"

The old woman sat back, resting her elbows on the worn arms of her chair. "He left her and the baby when Clara was six months old."

His fingers tightened around the handle of the mug. "What do you mean, he left her?"

"You should know the meaning. You did so yourself." She picked up her chocolate and held it in both hands. "I mean he packed his bags and left. She had the house—and the bills. He cleaned out the bank account and headed west."

"But he has a daughter."

"He hasn't laid eyes on the girl since she was in diapers. Faith pulled herself out. She had the child to think of after all if not herself. Her parents stood behind her. They're good people. She took a loan and started the doll business. We're proud to have her here."

He stared out the window to where the boughs of an old sycamore spread, dripping with snow and ice. "So I left, she married Tom, then he left. Seems Faith has a habit of picking the wrong men."

"Think so?"

He'd forgotten how dry her voice could be and nearly smiled. "Clara looks like Faith."

"Hmm. She favors her mother." The widow smiled into her mug. "I've always been able to see her father in her. Your chocolate's getting cold, Jason."

Absently, he sipped. With the taste came floods of memories. "I hadn't expected to feel at home here again. It's funny. I don't think I felt at home when I lived here, but now..."

"You haven't been by your old place yet?"

"No."

"There's a nice couple in there now. They put a porch on the back."

It meant nothing to him. "It was never home." He set the chocolate down and took her hand. "This was. I never knew any mother but you."

Her hand, thin, dry as paper, gripped his.

"Your father was a hard man, harder maybe because he lost your mother so young."

"I only felt relief when he died. I can't even be sorry for it. Maybe that's why I left when I did. With him gone, the house gone, it seemed the time was right."

"Maybe it was, for you. Maybe the time's right to come back again. You weren't a good boy, Jason. But you weren't so bad either. Give yourself some of that time you were always so desperate to beat ten years ago."

"And Faith?"

She sat back again. "As I recall, you never did much courting. Seems to me the girl chased after you with her eyes wide open. A man who's been all the places you been oughta know how to court a woman. Probably picked up some of those fancy languages."

He picked up a cookie and bit into it. "A phrase or two."

"Never knew a woman who wouldn't flutter a bit with some fancy language."

Leaning over he kissed both her hands. "I missed you."

"I knew you'd come back. At my age, you know how to wait. Go find your girl."

"I think I might." Rising, he slipped into his coat. "I'll come back and visit again."

"See that you do." She waited until he opened the door. "Jason—button your coat." She didn't pull out her handkerchief until she heard the door close behind him.

Chapter 4

The sun was high and bright when he stepped outside. Across the street a snowman was rapidly losing weight. He found the streets as he'd found them yesterday on his drive in—full of children fresh out of school. He felt the surge of freedom himself. As he headed north, he saw a girl break away from a group of children and come toward him. Even bundled in hat and scarf he recognized Clara.

"'Scuse me. Did you use to live here?"

"That's right." He wanted to tuck her hair into her cap but stopped himself.

"My mother said you did. Today in school,

the teacher said you went away and got famous."

He couldn't stop the grin. "Well, I went away."

"And you won a prize. Like Marcie's brother won a trophy for bowling."

He thought of his Pulitzer and managed, barely, not to laugh. "Something like that."

To Clara he looked like a regular person, not someone who bounded around the world on adventures. Her eyes narrowed. "Did you really go to all those places like they said?"

"That depends on what they said." In tacit agreement they began to walk together. "I've been to some places."

"Like Tokyo? That's the capital of Japan, we learned that in school."

"Like Tokyo."

"Did you eat raw fish?"

"Now and again."

"That's really disgusting." But she seemed pleased all the same. She bent and scooped up snow without breaking rhythm. "Do they squish grapes with their feet in France?"

"I can't say I ever saw it for myself, but I've heard tell."

"I sure wouldn't drink it after that. Did you ever ride a camel?"

He watched her bullet the snowball into the base of a tree. "As a matter of fact, I did."

"What was it like?"

"Uncomfortable."

It was a description she readily accepted because she'd already figured it out for herself. "The teacher read one of your stories today. The one about this tomb they found in China. Did you see the statues?"

"Yes, I did."

"Was it like *Raiders*?"

"Like what?"

"You know, the movie with Indiana Jones."

It took him a minute, then he laughed. Without thinking he tipped her cap over her eyes. "I guess it was, a little."

"You write good."

"Thank you."

They were standing on the sidewalk in front of her house. Jason glanced up, surprised. He hadn't realized they'd come so far and found himself regretting he hadn't slowed his pace a bit. "We have to do this report on Africa."

Clara wrinkled her nose. "It has to be five whole pages long. Miss Jenkins wants it in right after Christmas vacation."

"How long have you had the assignment?" It hadn't been that long since his school days.

Clara drew a circle in the snow at the edge of her lawn. "Couple of weeks."

No, he realized with some pleasure, it hadn't been so very long. "I guess you've started on it."

"Well, sort of." Then she turned that quick, beautiful smile on him. "You've been to Africa, haven't you?"

"A couple of times."

"I guess you know all kinds of things about climate and culture and stuff like that."

He grinned down at her. "Enough."

"Maybe you should stay for dinner tonight." Without giving him a chance to answer, she took his hand and led him around to the shop.

When they walked in, Faith was boxing a doll. Her hair was pinned up in the back and she wore a baggy sweatshirt over jeans. She was laughing at something her customer had said. "Lorna, you know you wouldn't have it any other way."

"Bah, humbug." The woman put a hand on her enormous stomach and sighed. "I really wanted this baby to make an appearance before Christmas."

"You still have four days."

"Hi, Mom!"

Faith turned to smile at her daughter. As she spotted Jason the spool of ribbon in her hand spun in a red stream to the floor. "Clara, you didn't wipe your feet," she managed to say, but kept her eyes on Jason.

"Jason! Jason Law." The woman rushed over and grabbed him by both arms. "It's Lorna—Lorna McBee."

He looked down into the pretty round face of his longtime neighbor. "Hello, Lorna." His gaze drifted down, then back up. "Congratulations."

With a hand on her stomach she laughed. "Thanks, but it's my third."

He thought of the scrawny, bad-tempered girl next door. "Three? You work fast."

"So does Bill. You remember Bill Easterday, don't you?"

"You married Bill?" He remembered a boy who had hung out in the town square looking for trouble. A few times Jason had helped him find it.

"I reformed him." When she smiled, he believed it. "He runs the bank." His expression had her giggling. "I'm serious, stop in sometime. Well, I've got to be moving along. This box has to go into a locked closet before my oldest girl sees it. Thanks, Faith, it's just lovely."

"I hope she likes it."

To keep her hands busy, Faith began to rewind the spool of ribbon. A puff of cold air came in, then was cut off as Lorna breezed out.

"Was that the bride doll?" Clara wanted to know.

"Yes, it was."

"Too fussy. Can I go over to Marcie's?"

"What about homework?"

"I don't have any except that dumb Africa report. He's going to help me." Jason met her smile with a lifted brow. "Aren't you?"

Jason would have dared any man within a hundred miles to resist that look. "Yes, I am."

"Clara, you can't—"

"It's okay 'cause I asked him to dinner." She beamed, almost sure her mother would be trapped by the good manners she was always talking about. "There's no school now for ten whole days so I can do the report after dinner, can't I?"

Jason decided it wouldn't hurt to apply a little pressure from his side. "I spent six weeks in Africa once. Clara might just get an A."

"She could use it," Faith muttered. They stood together, looking at her. Her heart already belonged to both of them. "I guess I'd better start dinner."

Clara was already racing across the yard next door before Faith pulled the door of the Doll House shut and turned the sign around to read Closed.

"I'm sorry if she was a nuisance, Jason. She has a habit of badgering people with questions."

"I like her," he said simply and watched Faith fumble with the latch.

"That's nice of you, but you don't have to feel obliged to help her with this report."

"I said I would. I keep my word, Faith." He touched a pin in her hair. "Sooner or later."

She had to look at him then. It was impossible not to. "You're welcome to dinner, of course." Her fingers worried the buttons of her coat as she spoke. "I was just going to fry chicken."

"I'll give you a hand."

"No, that's not—"

He cut her off when he closed his fingers over hers. "I never used to make you nervous."

With an effort, she steadied herself. "No, you didn't." He'd be gone again in a few days, she reminded herself. Out of her life. Maybe she should take whatever time she was given. "All right then, you can help."

He took her arm as they crossed the lawn. Though he felt her initial resistance, he ignored it. "I went to see Widow Marchant. I had cookies right from the oven."

Faith relaxed as she pushed open the door of her own kitchen. "She has every word you've ever written."

The kitchen was twice the size of the one

he'd just left and there were signs of a child
in the pictures hanging on the front of the re-
frigerator and a pair of fuzzy slippers kicked
into a corner. Moving with habit, Faith
switched on the burner under the kettle before
she slipped out of her coat. She hung it on a
peg by the door, then turned to take his. His
hands closed over hers.

"You didn't tell me Tom left you."

She'd known it wouldn't take him long to
hear it, or long to question. "It's not something I think about on a daily basis. Coffee?"

She draped his coat over a hook and turned
to find him blocking her way. "What happened, Faith?"

"We made a mistake." She said it calmly,
even coolly. It was a tone he'd never heard
from her before.

"But there was Clara."

"Don't." Fury came into her eyes quickly
and simmered there. "Leave it alone, Jason, I
mean it. Clara's my business. My marriage
and divorce are my business. You can't expect
to come back now and have all the answers."

They stood a moment, facing each other in

silence. When the kettle let out a whistle, she seemed to breathe again. "If you want to help, you can peel some potatoes. They're in the pantry over there."

She worked systematically, he thought angrily, as she poured oil to heat in a skillet and coated chicken. Her temper was nothing new to him. He'd felt the brunt of it before, sometimes deflecting it, sometimes meeting it head-on. He also knew how to soothe it. He began talking, almost to himself at first, about some of the places he'd been. When he told her about waking with a snake curled next to his head while he'd been camping in South America she laughed.

"I didn't find it too funny at the time. I was out of the tent in five seconds flat, buck naked. My photographer got a very interesting roll of pictures. I had to pay him fifty to get the negatives."

"I'm sure they were worth more. You didn't mention the snake in your series on San Salvador."

"No." Interested, he put down his paring knife. "You read it?"

She arranged chicken in the hot oil. "Of course. I've read all your stories."

He took the potatoes to the sink to wash them. "All of them?"

She smiled at the tone but kept her back to him. "Don't let your ego loose, Jason. It was always your biggest problem. I'd estimate that ninety percent of the people in Quiet Valley have read all your stories. You might say we all feel we have a stake in you." She adjusted the flame. "After all, no one else around here's had dinner at the White House."

"The soup was thin."

Chuckling, she put a pan of water on the stove and dumped in the potatoes. "I guess you just have to take the good with the bad—so to speak. I saw a picture of you a couple of years ago." She adjusted a pin in her hair and her voice was bland. "I think it was taken in New York, at some glitzy charity function. You had a half-naked woman on your arm."

He rocked back on his heels. "Did I?"

"Well, she wasn't actually half-naked," Faith temporized. "I suppose it just seemed that way because she had so much more hair than dress. Blond—very blond if my memory serves me. And let's say—top-heavy."

He ran his tongue around his teeth. "You meet a lot of interesting people in my business."

"Obviously." With the efficiency born of habit she turned chicken. Oil hissed. "I'm sure you find it very stimulating."

"Not as stimulating as this conversation."

"If you can't stand the heat," she murmured.

"Yeah. It's getting dark. Shouldn't Clara be home?"

"She's right next door. She knows to be home by five-thirty."

He went to the window anyway and glanced at the house next door. Faith studied his profile. It was stronger now, tougher. She supposed he was too, had had to be. How much was left of the boy she'd loved so desperately? Maybe it was something neither of them could be sure of.

"I thought of you a lot, Faith." Though his back was to her she could almost feel the words brush over her skin. "But especially at this time of year. I could usually block you out when I had work to do, deadlines to meet, but at Christmas you wouldn't let go. I remember every one we spent together, the way you'd drag me through the shops. Those few years with you made up for all the times as a kid I woke up to nothing."

The old sympathy welled up. "Your father couldn't face the holidays, Jason. He just couldn't handle it without your mother."

"I understand that better now. After losing you." He turned back. She wasn't looking at him now but bent industriously over the stove. "You've been spending Christmas alone, too."

"No, I have Clara."

She tensed as he walked to her. "No one to fill the stockings with you, or share secrets about what's under the tree."

"I manage. You have to alter life to suit yourself."

"Yeah." He took her chin in his hand. "I'm beginning to believe it."

The door slammed open. Wet and beaming, Clara stood dripping on the mat. "We made angels in the snow."

Faith raised a brow. "So I see. Well, you've got fifteen minutes to get out of those wet things and set the table."

She struggled out of her coat. "Can I turn on the tree?"

"Go ahead."

"Come on." Clara held out a hand for Jason. "It's the best one on the block."

Emotions humming, Faith watched them walk out together.

Chapter 5

They were still humming when the meal was over. She knew her daughter was a friendly, sometimes outrageously open child, but Clara had taken to Jason like a long lost friend. She chattered away at him as though she'd known him for years.

It's so obvious, Faith thought as she watched Clara stack dishes. Neither of them noticed. What would she do if they did? She didn't believe in lies, yet she'd been forced to live one.

The other two paid little attention to her as they settled down with Clara's books. In the easy, flowing style he'd been born with, Jason began to tell her stories about Africa—the desert, the mountains, the thick green jungle that teemed with its own life and its own dangers.

As their heads bent together over a picture in Clara's book Faith felt a flood of panic. "I'm going to go next door," she said on impulse. "I have a lot of work backed up."

"Mm-hmm." With that, Jason dismissed her. A laugh bubbled in her throat until it ached. Grabbing her coat, Faith escaped.

They were more than toys to her. They were certainly more than a business. To Faith the dolls who filled her shop were the symbol of youth, of innocence, of believing in miracles. She'd wanted to open the shop soon after Clara had been born, but Tom had been adamantly set against it. Because she'd felt indebted, she'd let it pass, as she'd let so many other things pass. Then when she'd found herself alone, with a child to support, it had seemed the natural thing.

She worked long hours there, to ease the void that even the love for her daughter couldn't fill.

In her workroom behind the store were shelves filled with pieces and parts of dolls. There were china heads, plastic legs and torsos. In another section lay the ones she called the sick and injured. Dolls with broken arms or battered bodies were brought to her for repair. Though she enjoyed selling and found a great creative thrill in making her own dolls, nothing satisfied her quite so much as taking a broken toy that was loved and making it whole again. She turned on the light and her radio and set to work.

It soothed her. As time passed, her nerves drained away. With crochet hook and rubber bands, with glue and painstaking care she replaced broken limbs. With a bit of paint and patience she brought smiles back to faceless dolls. Some were given new clothes or a fresh hairstyle, while others only needed a needle and thread plied by clever fingers.

By the time she picked up a battered rag doll she was humming.

"Are you going to fix that?"

Startled, she nearly stabbed herself with the needle. Jason stood in the doorway, hands in pockets, watching her. "Yes, that's what I do. Where's Clara?"

"She nearly fell asleep in her book. I put her to bed."

She started to rise. "Oh, well I—"

"She's asleep, Faith, with some green ball of hair she called Bernardo."

Determined to relax, Faith sat down again. "Yes, that's her favorite. Clara isn't much on ordinary dolls."

"Not like her mother?" Interested, he began to prowl the workroom. "I always thought when a toy broke or wore out it got tossed away."

"Too often. I've always thought that showed a tremendous lack of appreciation for something that's given you pleasure."

He picked up a soft plastic head, bald and smooth, that grinned at him. "Maybe you're right, but I don't see what can be done about that pile of rags in your hand."

"Quite a lot."

"Still believe in magic, Faith?"

She glanced up and for the first time her smile was completely open, her eyes warm.

"Yes, of course I do. Especially at Christmas-time."

Unable to help himself he reached down to run a hand over her cheek. "I said before that I'd missed you. I don't think I realized how much."

She felt the need shimmer and the longing plead inside her. Denying both, she concentrated on the doll. "I appreciate you helping Clara, Jason. I don't want to keep you."

"Does it bother you to have someone watch you work?"

"No." She began to replace stuffing. "Sometimes a concerned mother will stay here while I doctor a patient."

He leaned a hip against the counter. "I imagined a lot of things when I was coming back. I never imagined this."

"What?"

"That I'd be standing here watching you stuff life back into a rag. You may not have noticed, but it doesn't even have a face."

"It will. How did the report go?"

"She needs to do the final draft."

Faith glanced up from her work. Her eyes were wide with the joke. "Clara?"

"She had the same reaction." Then he smiled as he leaned back. The room smelled of her. He wondered if she knew. "She's a bright kid, Faith."

"Sometimes uncomfortably so."

"You're lucky."

"I know." With quick skillful movements, she pushed the stuffing into place.

"Kids love you no matter what, don't they?"

"No." She looked at him again. "You have to earn it." With needle and thread she began to secure the seams.

"You know, she was out on her feet, but she insisted on stopping at the tree to count the presents. She tells me she had this feeling there's going to be one more."

"I'm afraid she's doomed to disappointment. Her list looked like an army requisition. I had to draw the line." Putting down the thread, she picked up her paintbrush. "My parents already spoil her."

"They still live in town?"

"Mmm-hmm." She'd already gotten a sense of the doll's personality as she'd worked with it. Now, she began to paint it on. "They mumble about Florida from time to time, but I don't know if they'll ever go. It's Clara. They just adore her. You might go by and see them, Jason. You know my mother was always fond of you."

He examined a slinky red dress no bigger than his palm. "Your father wasn't."

She grinned at that. "He just didn't quite trust you." She sent him a quick, saucy smile. "What father would have?"

"He had good reason." As he walked toward her, he saw the doll she held. "I'll be damned." Charmed, he took it, holding it under the light. What had been a misshapen pile of rags was now a plump, sassy doll. Exaggerated lashes spiked out from wide eyes. Curls had been sewn back into place so that they fell teasingly over the brow. It was soft, friendly and pretty as a picture. Even a full grown man could recognize what would make a small girl smile.

She felt a ridiculous sense of accomplishment at seeing him smile at her work. "You approve?"

"I'm impressed. How much do you sell something like this for?"

"This one's not for sale." Faith set it in a large box at the back of the room. "There are about a dozen little girls in town whose families can't afford much of a Christmas. There are boys too, of course, but Jake over at the five-and-dime and I worked a deal a few years back. On Christmas Eve, a box is left on the doorstep. The girls get a doll, the boys a truck or a ball or whatever."

He should have known. It was so typical of her, so much what she was. "Santa lives."

She turned to smile at him. "He does in Quiet Valley."

It was the smile that did it. It was so open, so familiar. Jason closed the distance between them before either of them realized it.

"What about you? Do you get what you want for Christmas?"

"I have everything I need."

"Everything?" His hands cupped her face. "Aren't you the one who used to dream? Who always believed in wishes?"

"I've grown up. Jason, you should go now."

"I don't believe that. I don't believe you've stopped dreaming, Faith. Just being with you makes me start again."

"Jason." She pressed her hands to his chest, knowing she had to stop what could never be finished. "You know we can't always have what we want. You'll leave in a few days. You can walk away and go on to a hundred other things, a hundred other places."

"What does that have to do with right now? It's always right now, Faith." He drew his hands through her hair so that pins scattered. Rich warm sable tumbled over his fingers. He'd always loved the feel of it, the smell of it. "You're the only one," he murmured. "You've always been the only one."

She closed her eyes before he could draw her close. "You'll go. I have to stay here. Once before I stood and watched you walk away. I don't think I can bear it if I let you in again. Can't you understand?"

"I don't know. I know I understand I want you so much more now than I ever did. I'm not sure you can keep me out, Faith." But he backed away, for both of them. "Not for long anyway. You said before I didn't have a right to all the answers. Maybe that's true. But I need one."

It was a reprieve, it was space to think. She let out a long breath and nodded. "All right. But you promise that you'll go now if I answer?"

"I'll go. Did you love him?"

She couldn't lie. It wasn't in her. So her eyes were direct and pride kept her chin high. "I never loved anyone but you."

It came into his eyes—triumph, fury. He reached for her but she pulled away. "You said you'd go, Jason. I trusted your word."

She had him trapped. She had him aching. "You should've trusted it ten years ago." He swung from the workroom and into the frigid night.

Chapter 6

Quiet Valley bustled with Christmas energy. From a jerry-rigged loudspeaker on top of the hardware store roof carols rang out. An enterprising young man from a neighboring farm got a permit and gave buggy rides up and down Main Street. Kids, keyed up with lack of school and anticipation, shouted and raced on every corner. The skies had clouded over, but the snow held off.

Jason sat at the counter in the diner and sipped coffee while he listened to town gossip. Word was the Hennessys' oldest had the chicken pox and would be scratching himself through the holidays. Carlotta's was selling Christmas trees at half price and the hardware store had a sale on ten-speeds.

Ten years before Jason would have found the conversations mundane. Now he sat content, sipping his coffee and listening. Maybe this was what had been missing from the novel he'd been trying to write for so long. He'd been around the world, but everything had always been so fast paced, so urgent. There had been times when his life as well as his story had been on the line. You didn't think about it when it was happening. You couldn't. But now, sitting in the warm diner with the scent of coffee and frying bacon he could look back.

He'd taken assignments, a great many of them dangerous, because he hadn't given a damn. He'd already lost the part of himself he'd valued. It was true that over the years he'd built something back, inch by gritty inch, but he'd never found the whole—because he'd left it here, where he'd grown up. Now he just had to figure out what the hell to do with it.

"Guess they serve almost anybody in here."

Jason glanced up idly then grinned. "Paul.

Paul Tydings." His hand was gripped by two
enormous ones.

"Damn it, Jas, you're as good-looking and
skinny as ever."

Jason took a long look at his oldest friend.
Paul's hair was thick and curly around a full,
ruddy face offset now by a bushy moustache.
His bull-like frame had assured him a starting
place on the offensive line. Over the years, it
had thickened into what was politely termed
a successful build. "Well," Jason decided.
"You're as good-looking."

With a roar of laughter, Paul slapped him
on the back. "I never expected to see you back
here."

"Nor I you. I thought you were in Boston."

"Was. Made myself some money, got married."

"No kidding? How long?"

"Seven years come spring. Five kids."

Jason choked on his coffee. "Five?"

"Three and a set of twins. Anyway, I
brought my wife back for a visit six years ago
and she fell in love. Had a jewelry store in
Manchester, so I opened one here, too. I guess
I've got you to thank for a lot of it."

"Me? Why?"

"You were always filling my head with ideas. Then you took off. It made me think I should try my hand at seeing a few places. In about a year I was working in this jewelry store in Boston and in walks the prettiest little thing I ever laid eyes on. I was so flustered I never imprinted her credit card. She came back the next day with the blank receipt and saved my job. Then she saved my life and married me. Never even would have met her if it hadn't been for you talking about all the places there were to see." Paul nodded as his coffee was served. "Guess you've seen Faith."

"Yeah, I've seen her."

"Throw a lot of business her way being as three of my kids are girls and all of 'em are brats." He grinned and added two packages of sugar to his coffee. "She's as pretty as she was when she was sixteen and dancing in the town hall. Settling in this time, Jason?"

With a half laugh he pushed his cooling coffee aside. "Maybe."

"Come by the house and meet the family, will you? We're just south of town, the two-story stone place."

"I saw it driving in."

"Then don't go out again without coming in. A man doesn't have many friends who go back to red wagons with him, Jason. You know—" he glanced at his watch "—seems to me Faith breaks for lunch about now. I've got to get back." With a last slap on the back, Paul left him at the counter.

Thoughtfully, Jason sipped at his coffee. He'd been away ten years, a long time by any standard, yet everyone in town he ran into saw him and Faith as a couple. It seemed it was easy to blink away a decade. Easy for everyone, he added, but for himself and Faith. Maybe he could brush away the years, the time lost, but how could he ignore her marriage and her child?

He still wanted her. That hadn't changed. He still hurt. That hadn't eased. But how did she feel? She'd told him the night before that she'd never loved another man. Did that mean she still loved him? Jason dropped a bill on the counter and rose. There was only one way to find out. He'd ask her.

The Doll House was crowded with children. Noisy children. When Jason walked in shouts and laughter bounced off the walls. Helium-filled balloons hugged the ceiling and cookie crumbs littered the floor. In the doorway of the workroom was a tall cardboard castle. Just in front of a shiny white curtain stood a puppet of Santa Claus and a green-suited elf. With a lot of chatter and exaggerated effort, they loaded a glittering golden sleigh with colorful boxes. Twice the elf fell on his face while lifting a box and sent the children into peals of laughter. After a great deal of confusion, all the presents were loaded. With a belly-bursting *Ho-ho-ho!* Santa climbed into the sleigh. Bells jingling, it rocked its way through the curtain.

To the clatter of applause, a series of puppets crossed the stage for bows. Jason saw Mrs. Claus, two elves and a reindeer with a telltale red nose before Santa took the stage with a ringing *Merry Christmas!* He didn't even realize he was leaning back against the door and grinning when Faith popped around the castle for a bow of her own.

But she saw him. Feeling foolish, she took

another bow as the children clambered up. With the ease of a veteran kindergarten teacher, she maneuvered them toward the punch and cookies.

"Very impressive," Jason murmured in her ear. "I'm sorry I missed most of the show."

"It's not much." She combed her fingers through her hair. "I've been doing it for years now without much variation." She glanced over at the group of children. "It doesn't seem to matter."

"I'd say it does." He took her hand and brought it to his lips while a group of girls giggled. "Very much."

"Mrs. Monroe." A little boy with carrot-red hair and a face full of freckles tugged on her slacks. "When's Santa coming?"

Faith crouched down and smoothed at his hair. "You know, Bobby, I heard he was awfully busy this year."

His bottom lip poked out. "But he always comes."

"Well, I'm sure he'll find a way to get the presents here. I'm going to go in the back in a minute and see."

"But I have to talk to him."

The pout nearly did her in. "If he doesn't make it, you can give me a letter for him. I'll make sure he gets it."

"Problem?" Jason murmured when she straightened up again.

"Jake always plays Santa after the puppet show. We give out a few little things, it's nothing really, but the kids depend on it."

"Jake can't make it this year?"

"He caught the chicken pox from the Hennessy boy."

"I see." He hadn't celebrated Christmas in years, not since…since he'd left Faith. "I'll do it," he told her and surprised himself.

"You?"

Something in her expression made him determined to be the best St. Nick since the original. "Yeah, me. Where's the suit?"

"It's in the little room off the back, but—"

"I hope you remembered the pillows," he said before he sauntered away.

She didn't think he'd pull it off. In fact, five minutes after he walked away, Faith was sure he'd changed his mind altogether and continued out the back door. No one, including the group of kids with mouths full of cookies was more enchanted than she when Santa walked in the front door with a bag over his shoulder.

He had the chance for one booming *Merry Christmas* before he was surrounded. Too stunned to move, she watched the children bounce and jump and tug.

"Santa needs a chair." Jason sent her a long intense look that had her swallowing before her feet could move. Dashing into the back room, she brought out a high-backed chair and set it in the center of the room.

"Now you have to line up," she began, scooting children around. "Everyone gets a turn." Grabbing a bowl of candy canes, she set them on a table beside the chair. One by one, the children climbed up on Jason's knee. Faith needn't have worried. She'd had to school Jake to make the right responses, and most importantly, not to promise and risk disappointing. After the third child had climbed down, Faith relaxed. Jason was wonderful.

And having the time of his life. He'd done it just to help her out, perhaps even to impress her, but he got a great deal more. He'd never had a child sit on his lap and look at him with complete faith and love. He listened to their wishes, their confessions and complaints. Each one was allowed to reach in the sack he carried and pull out one gift.

He was hugged, kissed with sticky mouths and poked. One enterprising boy had a good grip on his beard before Jason managed to distract him. Happy, they began to file out of the shop with their parents or in groups.

"You were great." Faith turned her sign around after the last child had left to give herself a chance to catch her breath.

"Want to sit on my lap?"

Laughing, she walked to him. "I mean it, Jason, you were. I can't tell you how much I appreciate it."

"Then show me." He pulled her down onto his lap where she sank into pillows. She laughed again and kissed his nose.

"I've always been crazy about men in red suits. I wish Clara could have been here."

"Why wasn't she?"

With a little sigh, Faith let herself relax

against him. "She's too old for all this now—
so she tells me. She went shopping with Marcie."

"Nine's too old?"

She didn't speak for a minute, then moved
her shoulders. "Kids grow up fast." She
turned her head so she could look at him.
"You made a lot of them happy today."

"I'd like to make you happy." Reaching up,
he stroked her hair. "There was a time when
I could."

"Do you ever wish we could go back?"
Content, she let herself be cradled in his arms.
"When we were teenagers, everything seemed
so simple. Then you close your eyes for a minute and you're an adult. Oh, Jason, I wanted
you to carry me away, to a castle, to a moun-
taintop. I was so full of romance."

He continued to stroke her hair as they sat,
surrounded by dolls and the echo of children's
laughter. "I didn't have enough of it, did I?"

"You had your feet on the ground, I had
my head in the clouds."

"And now?"

"Now, I have a daughter to raise. It's terrifying sometimes to realize you're responsible for another life. Did you…?" She hesitated, knowing the ground was dangerous. "Did you ever want kids?"

"I haven't thought about it. Sometimes I have to go into places where it's tough enough being responsible for your own life."

She'd thought of that—had nightmares about it. "It still excites you."

He thought of some of the things he'd seen, the cruelty, the misery. "It stopped exciting me a long time ago. But I'm good at what I do."

"I suppose I always knew you would be. Jason." She shifted again so that her eyes were level with his. "I am glad you came back."

His fingers tightened when she rested her cheek against his. "You had to wait until I was stuffed like a walrus to tell me that."

With a laugh, she wrapped her arms around his neck. "It seems to be the safest time."

"Don't bet your life on it." He pressed his lips to hers and felt hers tremble. "What's so funny?"

Choking back the laugh, she drew away. "Oh nothing, nothing at all. I've always dreamed of being kissed by a man in a beard wearing a red hat and bells. I've got to clean up this mess."

When she rose, he hauled himself up. "The timing has to click sooner or later." She said nothing as she gathered up bits of colored paper. Jason picked up his sack and glanced inside. "There's one more box in here."

"It's for Luke Hennessy. Chicken pox."

He looked at the box, then back at her. Her hair curtained her face as she pulled a sticky candy cane from the carpet. "Where does he live?"

Still holding the candy, she stood up. Some might say he looked foolish, padded from chest to hips, wrapped in red and with his face half concealed by a curly white beard. Faith thought he'd never looked more wonderful. She walked to him to pull the beard down to his chin. Her arms went around him, her mouth found his.

Her kiss was warm as it always was, full of hope and simple goodness. Desire raced through him and settled into sweet contentment. "Thank you." She kissed him again in friendship. "He lives on the corner of Elm and Sweetbriar."

He waited a moment until he was steady. "Can I get a cup of coffee when I get back?"

"Yeah." She adjusted his beard again. "I'll be next door."

Chapter 7

He had to admit, it had given him a kick to walk through town. Kids flocked after him. Adults called out and waved. He was offered uncountable cookies. The biggest satisfaction had been the awe on the young Hennessy boy's face. That had topped the wide-eyed shock of his mother when she'd opened the door to S. Claus.

Jason took his time walking back, strolling through the square. It was strange, he discovered, how easy it was to take on the personality of a set of clothes. He felt...well, benevolent. If anyone he'd ever worked with had seen him now, they'd have fallen into the snow in a dead faint. Jason Law had a reputation for being impatient, brutally frank and quick-tempered. He hadn't won the Pulitzer for benevolence. Yet somehow, at the moment, he felt more satisfaction in the polyester beard and dime store bells than he did with all the awards he'd ever earned.

He was ho-hoing his way along when Clara stepped out of the five-and-dime. She and the little brunette at her side went off in peals of giggles.

"But you're—"

One narrow-eyed stare from Jason did the trick. Cutting herself off, Clara cleared her throat and offered her hand. "How do you do, Santa?"

"I do very well, Clara."

"That's not Jake," Marcie informed Clara. She stepped closer to try to recognize the face behind the puffs of white.

Enjoying himself, Jason sent her a wink. "Hello, Marcie."

The brunette's eyes widened. "How'd he know my name?" she whispered to her friend.

Clara covered another giggle with her hand. "Santa knows everything, don't you, Santa?"

"I have my sources."

"There isn't any Santa really." But Marcie's grown-up sophistication was wavering.

Jason leaned over and flicked at the fluffy ball on top of her cap. "There is in Quiet Valley," he told her and nearly believed it himself. He saw Marcie stop looking beyond the beard and accept the magic. Deciding against pressing his luck, he continued on down the street.

It wasn't easy for a fat man in a red suit to slip into a door inconspicuously, but Jason had had some experience. Once he was in the back room of Faith's shop, he shed the Santa clothes. He wanted to do it again. As Jason slipped into his own slim slacks, he realized he hadn't had so much fun in years. Part of it had been the look in Faith's eyes, the way she'd warmed to him, if only briefly. Part had been the simple act of giving pleasure. How long had it been since he'd done something without an angle? On an assignment there was constant bargaining. You give me this, I'll give you that. He'd had to toughen himself against sympathy, against compassion to find the truth and report it. If his style had a hard edge, it was because he'd always gone for the story that demanded it. It had helped him forget. Now that he'd come home it was impossible not to remember.

What kind of man was he really? He wasn't sure anymore, but he knew there was one woman who could make or break him. Leaving the suit in the closet, he went to find her.

She had been waiting for him. She was ready to admit she'd been waiting for him for ten years. Throughout the rest of the afternoon, Faith had made her own decisions. She'd made a success of her life. Though the search hadn't always been easy, she'd found contentment. Confidence had come with the years and she knew she could go on alone. It was time to stop being afraid of what her life would be like when Jason left again and to accept the gift she'd been offered. He was here, now, and she loved him.

When he came into the house he found her curled in a chair by the tree, her cheek resting on the arm. She waited until he came to her. "Sometimes at night I sit like this. Clara's asleep upstairs and the house is quiet. I can think about little things, enormous things, just as I did as a child. The lights all blend together and the tree smells like heaven. You can go anywhere, sitting just like this."

He picked her up, felt her yield, then settled in the chair with her on his lap. "I remember sitting like this with you at Christmastime in your parents' house. Your father grumbled."

She snuggled close. There was no padding now, just the long lean body she knew so well. "My mother dragged him into the kitchen so we could be alone for a little while. She knew you didn't have a tree at home."

"Or anything else."

"I never asked where you live now, Jason, whether you found a place that makes you happy."

"I move around a lot. I have a base in New York."

"A base?"

"An apartment."

"It doesn't sound like a home," she murmured. "Do you put a tree in the window at Christmas?"

"I guess I have once or twice, when I've been around."

It broke her heart, but she said nothing. "My mother always said you had wanderlust. Some people are born with it."

"I had to prove myself, Faith."

"To whom?"

"To myself." He rested his cheek on top of her head. "Damn it, to you."

She breathed in the scent of pine while the lights danced on the tree. They'd sat like this before, so long ago. The memories were nearly as sweet as the reality. "I never needed you to prove anything to me, Jason."

"Maybe that's one of the reasons I had to. You were too good for me."

"That's ridiculous." She would have shifted, but he held her still.

"You were, and still are." He too stared at

the tree. The tinsel shimmered in the lights like the magic he'd always wanted to give her. "Maybe that's why I had to leave when I did—maybe it's why I came back. You're all the good things, Faith. Just being with you brings out the best parts of me. God knows, there aren't many."

"You were always too hard on yourself. I don't like it." This time she did shift so that her hands were on his shoulders and her eyes were directly on his. "I fell in love with you. There were reasons for it. You were kind though you pretended not to be. You wanted to be considered tough and a troublemaker because you felt safer that way."

He smiled and ran a finger down her cheek. "I was a troublemaker."

"Maybe I liked that, too. You didn't just accept things, you weren't afraid to question."

"I nearly got kicked out of school twice because I questioned."

The old anger stirred. Had no one understood him but herself? Had no one else been able to see what had been racing and straining inside him? "You were smarter than anyone else. You've proved that if you needed to."

"You spent a lot of time defending me, didn't you?"

"I believed in you. I loved you."

He reached for her face in an old gesture that melted her heart. "And now?"

She had too much to say and not enough ways to say it. "Do you remember that night in June, after my Senior Prom? We drove out of town. The moon was full and the air was so sweet with summer."

"You wore a blue dress that made your eyes look like sapphires. You were so beautiful I was afraid to touch you."

"So I seduced you."

She looked so pleased with herself he laughed. "You did not."

"I certainly did. You would never have made love with me." She touched her lips to his. "Do I have to seduce you again?"

"Faith—"

"Clara's having dinner next door at Marcie's. She's going to spend the night. Come to bed with me, Jason."

Her quiet voice raced along his skin. The touch of her hand to his cheek seared like fire. But tangled with his need for her was a love that had never grown old. "You know I want you, Faith, but we're not children now."

"We're not children." She turned her face to press her lips into his palm. "And I want you. No promises, no questions. Love me the way you did on that one beautiful night we had together." Rising, she held out her hand. "I want something for the next ten years."

With their hands linked they walked up the stairs. He pushed away all thought of the other man she'd chosen, of the other life she'd lived. He, too, would block out ten years of loss and take what was offered.

Night came early in the winter so the light was dim. In silence she lit candles so that the room glowed gold and shifted with shadows. When she turned back to him she was smiling, with all the confidence and knowledge of a woman in her eyes. Saying nothing, she came to him, lifted her mouth and offered everything.

Her fingers were steady as she reached for the buttons of his shirt. His trembled as he reached for hers. Murmuring, she waited for the brush of his hands against her skin, then sighed from the sheer glory of it. They undressed each other slowly, not tentatively, but with the quiet understanding that every moment, every instant would be treasured.

When he saw her, as slim, as lovely, as unexplainably innocent as she'd been the first time, his head spun with needs, with doubts, with desires. But she stepped to him, pressed her body against his and dissolved all choices. She was stronger than she'd been. He could feel it, not in muscle but in spirit. Perhaps she had changed, but the longings that were racing through him were the same as they'd been in the boy on the brink of manhood. As heedlessly as the children they'd once been, they tumbled onto the bed.

They didn't relive the experience. It was as fresh, as wildly thrilling as the first time. But they were man and woman now, more demanding, hungrier. She drew him closer, run-

ning her hands over him with an urgency just
discovered, with a turbulence just released.
She'd waited so long, so very long and
wouldn't wait a moment longer.

But he took her hand and brought it to his
lips. He quieted her tumbling breath with his
mouth.

"I hardly knew what to do with you the first
time." Gently he nuzzled at her throat until
she moaned in frenzied anticipation. Raising
his head, he smiled at her. "Now I do."

Then he took her places she'd never been.
Higher, still higher he drew her, then just as
suddenly plunged her deep where the air was
thick and dark. Trapped in the whirlwind, she
clung. She'd wanted to give, but he left her
helpless. Tender, soft, easy, his fingers ca-
ressed until her body shuddered. He drank in
her sigh with lips abruptly urgent, ruthlessly
demanding, then patiently soothed her again.
Sensations rocketed inside her, leaving no
room for thought, for reason or even for memories.

When they came together it was everything

for both of them. Time didn't slip back but trapped them and held them close in the here and now.

He kept his arms tightly around her and they were quiet. With her eyes closed, she absorbed the unity. She loved, and for the moment there was nothing else. For him both ecstasy and contentment were troubled with questions. She was so warm, so free with her emotions. She loved him. He needed no words to know it and never had. But the loyalty he'd always understood as an intrinsic part of her had been broken. How could he rest without knowing why?

"I have to know why we lost ten years, Faith." When she said nothing, he turned her head toward him. Her eyes glistened in the shifting light but the tears didn't fall. "Now more than ever I have to know."

"No questions, Jason. Not tonight."

"I've waited long enough. We've waited long enough."

On a long breath, she sat up. Bringing her knees to her chest, she wrapped her arms

around them. Her hair cascaded down her
back. He couldn't resist taking a handful.
She'd been his once, completely. No one else
had ever touched her as he had. He knew he
had to accept her marriage, and that her child
belonged to another man, but he needed to
understand first why she had turned to someone else so soon after he'd gone away.

"Give me something, Faith. Anything."

"We loved each other, Jason, but we
wanted different things." She turned her head
to look at him. "We still want different
things." She took his hand and brought it to
her cheek. "If you had let me I would have
gone anywhere with you. I would have left my
home, my family and never looked back. You
needed to go alone."

"I didn't have anything for you," he began.
She stopped him with a look.

"You never gave me a choice."

He reached for her once more. "If I gave
you one now?"

She closed her eyes and let her forehead rest
on his. "Now I have a child, and she has a

home I can't take away from her. What I want
doesn't come first." She drew back far enough
to look at him. "What you want can't come
first. Before somehow I never thought you'd
really go. This time I know you will. Let's just
take what we have, give each other this one
Christmas. Please."

She closed her mouth over his and stopped
all questions.

Chapter 8

Christmas Eve was magic. Faith had always believed it. When she awoke with Jason beside her, it was more than magic. For a while, she simply lay there, watching him sleep. She'd imagined it before, as a girl, as a woman, but now she didn't need the dreams. He was here beside her, warm, quiet, and outside an early morning snow was falling. Careful not to wake him, Faith slipped out of bed.

When he rolled over, he smelled her—the springtime scent her hair had left on the pillowcase. For a few minutes, he lay still and let it seep into his system. Content, he lay back and looked at the room he hadn't been able to see in the dark.

The walls were papered, ivory, with little sprigs of violets. At the windows were fussy priscillas. There was an antique rosewood bureau cluttered with colored bottles and boxes. On a vanity was an old-fashioned silver-handled brush and comb. He watched the snow fall and smelled the potpourri on the stand beside the bed. The room was so like her—charming, fresh, and very, very feminine. A man could relax there even knowing he might find stockings draped over a chair or a blouse mixed with his shirts. He could relax there. And he wasn't letting her go again.

He smelled the coffee before he was halfway down the stairs. She had Christmas music on the stereo and bacon frying. He hadn't known it would feel so good just to walk into a kitchen and find your woman cooking for you.

"So you're up." She was wrapped from head to foot in a bright flannel robe. Desire dragged quietly at his stomach muscles. "There's coffee."

"I could smell it." He went to her. "I could smell you the moment I woke."

She rested her head on his shoulder, trying not to think that this was the way it might have been—if only. "You look as though you could have slept for hours. It's a good thing you didn't or the bacon would be cold."

"If you'd stayed in bed a few more minutes, we might have—"

"Mom! Mom! It's snowing!" Clara burst through the door and danced around the kitchen. "We're going to go caroling tonight in the hay wagon and there's snow all over the place." She stopped in front of Jason and grinned. "Hi."

"Hi yourself."

"Mom and I are going to build a snowman. She says Christmas snowmen are the best. You can help."

She hadn't known just what reaction Clara would have to finding Jason at the breakfast table. With a shake of her head, Faith began to beat eggs. She should have known Clara would be willing to accept anyone she'd decided to like. "You have to have some breakfast."

Clara fingered the plastic Santa on her lapel, tugging on the string so that the nose lit up. It never failed to please her. "I had cereal at Marcie's."

"Did you thank her mother for having you?"

"Yeah." She stopped a minute. "I think I did. Anyway we're going to build two of them and have a wedding and everything. Marcie wanted the wedding," she added to Jason.

"Clara would prefer a war."

"I figured we could have that after. Maybe I should have some hot chocolate first." She eyed the cookie jar and calculated her chances. Slim at best.

"I'll fix it. And you can have a cookie after the snowman," Faith told her without bothering to turn. "Hang your things by the door."

Scrambling out of her coat, she chattered at Jason. "You're not going back to Africa, are you? I don't think Africa would be much fun at Christmas. Marcie's mother said you'd probably be going to some other neat place."

"I'm supposed to go to Hong Kong in a few weeks." He glanced at Faith. She didn't turn. "But I'll be around for Christmas."

"Do you have a tree in your room?"

"No."

She gave him a wide-eyed look. "Well, where do you put your presents? It's not Christmas without a tree, is it, Mom?"

Faith thought of the years Jason had grown up without one. She remembered how hard he'd tried to pretend it didn't matter. "A tree's only so that we can show other people it's Christmas."

Unconvinced, Clara plopped into a chair. "Well, maybe."

"She used to say the same thing to me," Jason told Clara. "In any case, I don't think Mr. Beantree would like it if I left pine needles all over the floor."

"We've got a tree, so you can have dinner with us," Clara declared. "Mom makes this big turkey and Grandma and Grandpa come over. Grandma brings pies and we eat till we're sick."

"Sounds great." Amused, he looked over as Faith scooped eggs onto a plate. "I had Christmas dinner with your grandparents a couple of times."

"Yeah?" Interested, Clara studied him. "I guess I heard somewhere that you used to be Mom's boyfriend. How come you didn't get married?"

"Here's your hot chocolate, Clara." Faith set it down. "You'd better hurry, Marcie's waiting."

"Are you coming out?"

"Soon." Grateful that her daughter was easily distracted, she set the platter of bacon and eggs on the table. Ignoring the half-amused lift of brow from Jason, she took her seat.

"We need carrots and scarves and stuff."

"I'll take care of it."

With a grin Clara gulped down chocolate. "And hats?"

"And hats."

A snowball hit the kitchen window. Clara was up like a shot. "There she is. Gotta go. Come soon, Mom, you make the best."

"Soon as I'm dressed. Don't forget your top button."

Clara hesitated at the back door. "I've got a little plastic tree in my room. You can have it if you want."

Moved, he only stared at her. Just like her mother, he thought, and fell in love a second time. "Thanks."

"'Sokay. Bye."

"She's quite a kid," Jason commented as the door slammed behind her.

"I like her."

"I'll give her a hand with the snowman."

"You don't have to, Jason."

"I want to, then I've got some things to take care of." He checked his watch. It was only Christmas Eve for so long. When a man was being offered a second chance, it wasn't wise to waste time. "Can I get an invitation for tonight?"

Faith smiled but simply pushed the food around on her plate. "You've never needed one."

"Don't cook, I'll bring something."

"It's okay, I—"

"Don't cook," he repeated, rising. He bent to kiss her, then lingered over it. "I'll be back."

He took his coat from the hook where it had hung beside Clara's. When he was gone,

Faith looked down at the toast she'd crumbled in her hand. Hong Kong. At least this time she knew where he was going.

The snow people in the side yard grinned at him as he struggled past. Boxes balanced, Jason knocked on the back door with the toe of his boot. The snow hadn't let up a whit.

"Jason." Speechless, Faith stepped back as he teetered inside.

"Where's Clara?"

"Clara?" Still staring, she pushed back her hair. "She's upstairs getting ready for the hayride."

"Good. Take the top box."

"Jason, what in the world have you got here?"

"Just take the top box unless you want pizza all over the floor."

"All right, but..." As the enormous box in his arms shifted, she laughed. "Jason, what have you done?"

"Wait a minute."

Holding the pizza, she watched him drag the box into the living room. "Jason, what is that thing?"

"It's a present." He started to set it under the tree then discovered there wasn't enough room. With a bit of rearranging, he managed to lean the box against the wall beside the tree. He was grinning when he turned to her. If he'd ever felt better in his life, he couldn't remember it. "Merry Christmas."

"Same to you. Jason, what is that box?"

"Damn, it's cold out there." Though he rubbed his hands together now, he hadn't even noticed the biting wind. "Got any coffee?"

"Jason."

"It's for Clara." He discovered that feeling a bit foolish didn't dim the warmth.

"You didn't have to get her a present," Faith began, but her curiosity got the better of her. "What is it?"

"This?" Jason patted the six-foot box. "Oh, it's nothing."

"If you don't tell me you don't get any coffee." She smiled. "And I keep the pizza."

"Spoilsport. It's a toboggan." He took Faith's arm to lead her out of the room. "She happened to mention when we were building the snowman that some kid had this toboggan and it went down Red Hill like a spitfire."

"Spitfire," Faith murmured.

"And snow like this is just made for going down Red Hill like a spitfire, so…"

"Sucker," Faith accused and kissed him hard.

"Put that pizza down and call me that again."

She laughed and kept it between them.

"Wow!"

Faith raised a brow at the noise from the living room. "I think she saw the box."

At full speed, Clara barreled into the kitchen. "Did you see? I knew there'd be one more, I just knew. It's as tall as you are," she told Jason. "Did you see?" She grabbed his hand to drag him back. "It has my name on it."

"Imagine that." Jason picked her up and kissed both cheeks. "Merry Christmas."

"I can't wait." She threw her arms around his neck and squeezed. "I just can't wait."

Watching them, Faith felt her emotions tangle and knot until her bones ached with it.

What should she do? What could she do?
When Jason turned with Clara, the lights from
the tree fell like wishes over their faces.

"Faith?" He didn't need words to recognize
distress, pain, turmoil. "What is it?"

Her hands were digging into the cardboard
of the box. "Nothing. I'm going to dish out
this pizza before it's cold."

"Pizza?" Delighted, Clara bounced down.
"Can I have two pieces? It's Christmas."

"Monkey," Faith scolded gently, tousling
her hair. "Set the table."

"What is it, Faith?" Jason took her arm before she could follow her daughter into the
kitchen. "Something's wrong."

"No." She had to control herself. She'd
managed everything for so long. "You overwhelmed me." With a smile she touched his
face. "It's happened before. Come on, let's
eat."

Because she seemed to need to keep her
thoughts to herself, he let it go and followed
her into the kitchen where Clara was already
peeking into the cardboard box. He'd never
seen a child plow through food with such un-

restrained glee. He'd never known Christmas Eve could be special simply because there was someone beside him.

Clara swallowed the last of her second piece. "Maybe if I opened one present tonight there'd be less confusion in the morning."

Faith seemed to consider. "I like confusion," she decided and Jason realized the conversation was an old tradition.

"Maybe if I opened just one present tonight, I could get right to sleep. Then you wouldn't have to wait so long to creep around and fill the stockings."

"Hmm." Faith pushed aside her empty plate and enjoyed the wine Jason had brought. "I like creeping around late at night."

"If I opened—"

"Not a chance."

"If I—"

"Nope."

"But Christmas is just hours and hours away."

"Awful, isn't it?" Faith smiled at her. "And you're going caroling in ten minutes, so you'd better get your coat."

Clara walked over to tug on her boots. "Maybe when I get back, there'll be just one present that you'll figure isn't really important enough to wait until morning."

"All the presents under the tree are absolutely vital." Faith rose to help her on with her coat. "And so are the following instructions. Stay with the group. Keep your mittens on; I want you to keep all your fingers. Don't lose your hat. Remember that Mr. and Mrs. Easterday are in charge."

"Mom." Clara shifted her feet and sighed. "You treat me like a baby."

"You are my baby." Faith gave her a smacking kiss. "So there."

"Jeez, I'll be ten years old in February. That's practically tomorrow."

"And you'll still be my baby in February. Have a good time."

Clara sighed, long-suffering and misunderstood. "Okay."

"Okay," Faith mimicked. "Say goodnight."

Clara peeked around her mother. "Are you going to stay until I get back?"

"Yeah."

Satisfied, she grinned and pulled open the door. "Bye."

"Monster," Faith declared and began to stack plates.

"She's terrific." Standing, Jason helped clear the clutter. "Little for her age, I guess. I didn't realize she was almost ten. It's hard to—" He stopped as Faith clattered dishes in the sink. "She'll be ten in February."

"Umm. I can't believe it myself. Sometimes it seems like yesterday, and then again..." She trailed off, abruptly breathless. With studied care, she began to fill the sink with soapy water. "I'll just be a minute here if you'd like to take your wine into the living room."

"In February." Jason took her arm. When he turned her, he saw the blood drain from her face. His fingers tightened, bruising without either of them noticing. "Ten years in February. We made love that June. God, I don't know how many times that night. I never touched you again, we never had the chance to be alone like that again before I left, just a few weeks later. You must have married Tom in September."

Her throat was dry as bone. She couldn't even swallow, but stared at him.

"She's mine," he whispered and it vibrated through the room. "Clara's mine."

She opened her mouth to speak, but there seemed to be nothing she could say. Lips trembling, eyes drenched, she nodded.

"God!" He had her by both arms, nearly lifting her off her feet before he backed her into the counter. The fury in his eyes would have made her cringe if she hadn't been willing to accept it. "How could you? Damn you, she's ours and you never told me. You married another man and had our baby. Did you lie to him, too? Did you make him think she was his so you could have your cozy house and lace curtains?"

"Jason, please—"

"I had a right." He thrust her away before he could give into the violence that pushed him on. "I had a right to her. Ten years. You stole that from me."

"No! No it wasn't like that. Jason, please! You have to listen!"

"The hell with you." He said it calmly, so

calmly she stepped back as though she'd been slapped. The anger she could argue with, even reason with. Quiet rage left her helpless.

"Please, let me try to explain."

"There's nothing you can say that could make up for it. Nothing." He yanked his coat from the wall and stormed out.

"You're a damn fool, Jason Law." The Widow Marchant sat in her kitchen rocker and scowled.

"She lied to me. She's been lying for years."

"Hogwash." She fiddled with the tinsel on the little tree on the stand by the window. Cheerful strains from the Nutcracker floated in from the living room. "She did what she had to do, nothing more, nothing less."

He prowled around the room. He still wasn't sure why he'd come there instead of heading for Clancy's Bar. He'd walked in the snow for an hour, maybe more, then found himself standing on the widow's doorstep. "You knew, didn't you? You knew I was Clara's father."

"I had my ideas." The rocker squeaked

gently as she moved. "She had the look of
you."

That brought a peculiar thrill, one he didn't
know what to do with. "She's the image of
Faith."

"True enough if you don't look hard. The
eyebrows are you, and the mouth. The sweet
Lord knows the temperament is. Jason, if
you'd known you were to be a father ten years
back, what would you have done?"

"I'd have come back for her." He turned,
dragging a hand through his hair. "I'd have
panicked," he said more calmly. "But I'd have
come back."

"I always thought so. But it—well, it's
Faith's story to tell. You'd best go on back and
hear it."

"It doesn't matter."

"Can't stand a martyr," she muttered.

He started to snap, then sighed instead. "It
hurts. It really hurts."

"That's life for you," she said not unsym-
pathetically. "Want to lose them both again?"

"No. God, no. But I don't know how much
I can forgive."

The old woman raised both brows. "Fair enough. Give Faith the same courtesy."

Before he could speak again, the kitchen door burst open. In the doorway stood Faith, covered with snow, face washed with tears. Ignoring the wet she brought in with her, she ran to Jason. "Clara," she managed to stammer.

When he took her arms he felt the shudders. Terror flowed from her into him. "What's happened?"

"She's missing."

Chapter 9

"They're going to find her." Jason held her arm as they both stumbled through the snow to her car. "They probably have already."

"One of the kids said he thought she and Marcie went behind this farmhouse to look at the horses in the barn. But when they went back, they weren't there. It's dark." Faith fumbled with her keys.

"Let me drive."

She gave him no argument as she climbed in the passenger side. "Lorna and Bill called the sheriff from the farmhouse. Half the town's out there looking for them. But there's so much snow, and they're just little girls. Jason—"

He took her face in his hands, firmly. "We're going to find them."

"Yes." She wiped away tears with the heels of her hands. "Let's hurry."

He couldn't risk more than thirty miles an hour. They crept down the snow-covered road, searching the landscape for any sign. The hills and fields lay pristine and undisturbed. To Faith they looked unrelenting. But while fear still overwhelmed her, she'd conquered the tears.

Ten miles out of town the fields were lit up like noonday. Groups of cars crisscrossed the road and men and women tramped through the snow calling. Jason had barely stopped when Faith was out and running toward the sheriff.

"We haven't found them yet, Faith, but we will. They won't have gone far."

"You've searched the barn and the outbuildings?"

The sheriff nodded at Jason. "Every inch."

"How about in the other direction?"

"I'm going to send some men that way."

"We'll go now."

The snow was blinding as he weaved through the other cars. He slackened his speed even more and started to pray. He'd been on a search party once in the Rockies. He hadn't forgotten what a few hours in the wind and snow could do.

"I should have made her wear another sweater." Faith gripped her hands together in her lap as she strained to see out the window. In her hurry she'd forgotten her gloves but didn't notice her numb fingers. "She hates it so when I fuss and I didn't want to spoil the evening for her. Christmas is so special for Clara. She's been so excited." Her voice broke as a ripple of fear became a wave. "I should have made her wear another sweater. She'll be— *Stop!*"

The car fishtailed as he hit the brakes. It took every ounce of control for him to deal with the swerve. Faith pushed open the door and stumbled out. "Over there, it's—"

"It's a dog." He had her by the arms before she could run across the empty field. "It's a dog, Faith."

"Oh, God." Beyond control, she collapsed against him. "She's just a little girl. Where could she be? Oh, Jason, where is she? I should have gone with her. If I'd been there she—"

"Stop it!"

"She's cold and she must be frightened."

"And she needs you." He gave her a quick shake. "She needs you."

Struggling for control, she pressed a hand to her mouth. "Yes. Yes, I'm all right. Let's go. Let's go a little further."

"You wait in the car. I'm going to walk across this field for a bit and see if I spot something."

"I'll go with you."

"I can move faster alone. I'll only be a few minutes." He started to urge her toward the car when a flash of red caught his eye. "Over there."

He gripped her arm as he tried to see through the snow. Just at the edge of the field, he saw it again.

"It's Clara." Faith was already struggling away. "She has a red coat." Snow kicked up around her as she ran. It fell cold and wet to mix with the tears that blinded her vision. With all the breath she had she called out. Arms spread wide, she caught both girls to her. "Oh God, Clara, I've been so scared. Here, here now, you're frozen, both of you. We'll get to the car. Everything's going to be fine. Everything's all right now."

"Is my mom mad?" Shivering, Marcie wept against her shoulder.

"No, no, she's just worried. Everyone is."

"Up you go." Jason hauled Clara up in his arms. For one brief minute he gave himself the luxury of nuzzling his daughter. Looking back, he saw Faith gathering up Marcie. "Can you manage?"

She smiled, holding the still weeping girl close. "No problem."

"Then let's go home."

"We didn't mean to get lost." Clara's tears ran down his collar.

"Of course you didn't."

"We just went to look at the horses and we got all turned around. We couldn't find anybody. I wasn't scared." Her breath hitched as she pressed against him. "Just Marcie."

His child. He felt his own vision blur as he wrapped his arms tighter around her. "You're both safe now."

"Mom was crying."

"She's okay, too." He stopped at the car. "Can you handle them both on your lap in the front? They'll be warmer."

"Absolutely." After Faith had settled in with Marcie, Jason handed her Clara. For one long moment, their gazes held over her head.

"We couldn't find the lights of the house with all the snow," Clara murmured as she held on to her mother. "Then we couldn't find the road for the longest time. It was so cold. I didn't lose my hat."

"I know, baby. Here, get your wet mittens off. You, too, Marcie. Jason has the heater turned all the way up. You'll be cooked before you know it." She ran kisses over two cold faces and fought the need to break down. "What Christmas carols did you sing?"

"'Jingle Bells,'" Marcie said with a sniffle.

"Ah, one of my favorites."

"And 'Joy to the World,'" Clara put in. The heater was pumping warm air over her hands and face. "You like that one better."

"So I do but I can't remember just how it starts. How does it start, Marcie?" She smiled at Clara and snuggled her closer.

In a thin, piping voice still wavery with tears Marcie started to sing. She was nearly through the first verse when they came to the rest of the search party.

"It's my dad!" Bouncing on Faith's lap, Marcie started to wave. "He doesn't look mad."

With a half laugh, Faith kissed the top of her head. "Merry Christmas, Marcie."

"Merry Christmas, Mrs. Monroe. See you tomorrow, Clara." Marcie barely had time to open the door before she was scooped up.

"What a night." There were waves and cheers as the car weaved through the crowd.

"It's Christmas Eve," Clara reminded her mother. The world was safe and warm again. "Maybe I should open that one big present tonight."

"Not a chance," Jason told her and tugged at her hair.

Faith turned Clara in her arms and squeezed tight.

"Don't cry, Mom."

"I have to, for just a minute." True to her word, her eyes were dry when they arrived home. An exhausted Clara dozed on Jason's shoulder as he carried her inside. "I'll take her up, Jason."

"We'll take her up."

She let her arms fall back to her sides and nodded.

They pulled off boots and socks and sweaters and wrapped Clara in warm flannel. She murmured a bit and tried to stay awake but the adventures of the evening took their toll. "It's Christmas Eve," she mumbled. "I'm going to get up real early in the morning."

"As early as you like," Faith told her as she pressed a kiss to her cheek.

"Can I have cookies for breakfast?"

"Half a dozen," Faith agreed recklessly. She smiled and was asleep before Faith pulled the blankets around her.

"I was afraid..." She let her hand linger on her daughter's cheek. "I was afraid I'd never see her like this again. Safe, warm. Jason, I don't know how to thank you for just being

there. If I'd been alone—" She broke off and
shook her head.

"I think we should go downstairs, Faith."

The tone made her press her lips together.
She'd be ready, she promised herself, to handle the accusations, the bitterness, the resentment. "I think I'd like a drink," she said as
they walked downstairs. "Some brandy. It
looks like the fire's gone out."

"I'll take care of it. You get the brandy.
There are some things I have to say."

"All right." She left him to go to the little
cabinet in the dining room. When she came
back, the fire was just catching. He straightened from it and took a snifter.

"Do you want to sit down?"

"No, I can't." She sipped, but it would have
taken more than brandy to steady her nerves.
"Whatever you have to say, Jason, you should
say it."

Chapter 10

She stood looking at him, her back straight, her eyes burning with emotion, her hands clasping the snifter tightly. Part of him wanted to go to her, gather her close and just hold on. He'd found a child and nearly lost her in the same night. Did anything else matter? But inside was a void that had to be filled. Questions, demands, accusations had to be answered. There had to be an accounting before there could be understanding, and understanding before there could be forgiveness. But where did he start?

He walked to the tree. There was a star on

top that shed silver light over all the other colors. "I'm not sure I know what to say. It isn't every day a man turns around and finds himself with a half-grown daughter. I feel cheated out of watching her learn to walk, hearing her talk, Faith. Nothing you can do or say can ever give that back to me, can it?"

"No."

He turned to see her holding the brandy at waist level. Her face was very pale and calm. Whatever emotions she was feeling she managed to restrain. Yes, this was a different Faith than the one he'd left. The girl would never have been able to exert the self-control the woman did. "No excuses, Faith?"

"I guess I thought I had them, then tonight when I thought I'd lost her..." Her voice trailed off and she shook her head. "No excuses, Jason."

"She thinks Tom's her father."

"No!" Her eyes weren't calm now but brilliant. "Do you think I'd let her believe her father had deserted her, that he didn't care enough even to write? What she knows is basically the truth. I never lied to her."

"What is the truth?"

She took a steadying breath. When she looked at him her face was still pale but her voice was calm again. "That I loved her father, and he loved me, but he had to go away before he even knew about her and he wasn't able to come back."

"He would have."

Something rushed into her eyes but she turned away. "I told her that, too."

"Why?" The fury came back and he fought against it. "I have to know why you did what you did. I lost all those years."

"You?" Her temper was less easily controlled than her grief. Years of holding back bubbled inside her and burst out. "*You* lost?" she repeated as she whirled around. "You were gone and I was eighteen years old, pregnant and alone."

Guilt flared. He hadn't expected it. "I wouldn't have left if you'd told me."

"I didn't know." She put the brandy down and pushed back her hair with both hands. "It was just a week after you'd gone that I found out I was carrying our baby. I was thrilled."

With a laugh, she wrapped her arms around her chest. For a moment she looked heart-breakingly young and innocent. "I was so happy. I waited every day, every night for you to call so I could tell you." Her eyes sobered. The smile faded. "But you never called, Jason."

"I needed time to set things up—a steady job, a place I could ask you to live in."

"You never understood it didn't matter where I lived, as long as it was with you." She shook her head before he could speak. "It doesn't matter now. That part's over. A week passed, then two, then a month. I got ill, just tension, morning sickness, but I began to realize you weren't going to call. You weren't coming back. I was angry for a while, acknowledging you just hadn't wanted me enough. Small-town girl."

"That's not true. That was never true."

She studied him a moment, almost dispassionately. The lights of the tree fell over his dark-blond hair, glimmered in the deep, deep eyes that had always held their own secrets. Restlessness. "Wasn't it?" she murmured. "It was certainly true that you wanted out. I was part of Quiet Valley and you wanted out."

"I wanted you with me."

"But not enough to let me go with you." She shook her head when he started to speak. "Not enough to let me come to you until you'd proved the things you needed to prove. I didn't always understand that, Jason, but I began to when you came back."

"You weren't ever going to tell me about Clara, were you?"

She heard the bitterness again and closed her eyes against it. "I don't know. I honestly don't."

He drank, hoping it would warm the ice in his veins. "Tell me the rest."

"I wanted the baby, but I was scared, too scared even to tell my mother."

She picked up the brandy again but merely warmed her hands with it. "I should have of course, but I wasn't thinking clearly."

"Why did you marry Tom?" But even as he asked, he realized the old jealousies were fading. He only wanted to understand.

"Tom would come by almost every night.

We'd talk. He didn't seem to mind me talking about you and God knows I needed to. Then one night we were sitting on the porch and I just broke down. I was three months pregnant and my body was changing. That morning I hadn't been able to snap my jeans." With a shaky laugh, she ran a hand over her face. "It sounds so silly, but I hadn't been able to snap my jeans and it was terrifying. It made me realize there was no going back. Everything just poured out while we sat there. He said he'd marry me. Of course I said no, but he began to reason it all out. You weren't coming back and I was pregnant. He loved me and wanted to marry me. The baby would have a name, a home, a family. It sounded so right the way he said it and I wanted the baby to be safe. I wanted to be safe."

She drank now because her throat ached. "It was wrong, right from the beginning. He knew I didn't love him, but he just wanted me, or thought he did. The first few months he tried, we both really tried. But after Clara came, he couldn't handle it. I could see every time he looked at her he thought of you. There was nothing I could do to change the fact that she was yours." She paused and found it easier to say it all. "There was nothing I would have done to change that. As long as I had her, I had part of you. Tom knew it, no matter how much I tried to be what he wanted. He started drinking, picking fights, staying out. It was as though he wanted me to ask for a divorce."

"But you didn't."

"I didn't because I...well, I felt I owed him. Then one day I came home from taking Clara out and he was gone. Divorce papers came in the mail, and that was that."

"Why didn't you ever try to contact me, Faith, through one of the magazines or newspapers?"

"And say what? Jason, remember me? By the way, you have a daughter back here in Quiet Valley. Drop in some time."

"One word—one word from you and I'd have left everything and come back. I never stopped loving you."

She closed her eyes. "I watched you walk away from me. I watched you get on the bus and leave me without a trace. I stood there for hours, half believing you'd get off at the next stop and come back. I was the one who had to stay behind, Jason."

"I called. Damn it, Faith, it only took me six months to get something started."

She smiled. "And when you called I was seven months pregnant. My mother didn't tell me for a long time, not until after Tom had left. She said you made her promise."

"I needed my pride."

"I know."

That she didn't question. He saw the way she smiled as she said it, as if she'd always understood. "You must have been terrified."

Her smile softened. "There were moments."

"You must have hated me."

"Never. How could I? You went away but you left me with the most beautiful thing in my life. Maybe you were right, maybe I was. Maybe we were both wrong, but there was Clara. Every time I looked at her, I could remember how much I loved you."

"How do you feel now?"

"Shaky." She laughed a little, then folded her hands, determined to do what was right.

"Clara should be told. I'd prefer doing it my-self."

The idea made him reach for the brandy again. "How do you think she'll take it?"

"She's learned to get along without a father. It doesn't mean she hasn't needed one." She sat up straight and raised her chin. "You have a right, of course, to see her whenever you like, but I won't have her bounced around. I also realize you can't be here for her all the time because of your work, but don't think you can just pop into her life and out again. You'll have to make an effort, to keep in touch with her Jason."

So this was another fear she'd lived with, he realized. Maybe he deserved it. "You don't trust me, do you?"

"Clara's too important." She let out a little sigh. "So are you."

"If I told you I fell for her before I knew, would it make a difference?"

She thought of the toboggan, of the way he'd looked when Clara had thrown her arms around his neck. "She needs all the love she can get. We all do. She's so much like you,

I—" She broke off when her eyes filled. "Damn, I don't want to do this." Impatient, she brushed tears away. "I'll tell her tomorrow, Jason. On Christmas. You and I can work out the arrangements. I know you're leaving soon, but if you could stay a few more days, give her some time, it would make it easier for all of us."

He rubbed at the tension at the back of his neck. "You never asked me for much of anything, did you?"

She smiled. "I asked you for everything. We were both too young to realize it."

"You always believed in magic, Faith." He pulled a box out of his pocket. "It's nearly midnight. Open it now."

"Jason." She pushed her hands through her hair. How could he think of presents now? "I don't think this is the time."

"It's ten years past time."

When he thrust the box at her she found herself gripping it with both hands. "I don't have anything to give you."

He touched her face, almost hesitantly. "You've just given me a daughter."

Relief poured through her. Instead of bitterness, she heard gratitude. Love, never dimmed, shimmered in her eyes. "Jason—"

"Please, open it."

She pulled off the glossy red paper and revealed the black velvet box beneath. With fingers not quite steady she opened it. The ring was a teardrop, frozen in place, glorious with the reflected lights from the tree.

"Paul told me it was the best he had."

"You bought this before you knew—"

"Yeah, before I knew I was going to ask the mother of my child to marry me. We'll be legal, the three of us." He took her hand and waited. "How about a second chance? I won't let you down, Faith."

"You never did." Close to tears again, she reached out her hand to his cheek. "It wasn't you, it wasn't me, it was life. Oh, Jason, I want this. Understand, all I've ever really wanted was to be married to you, have a family with you."

"Then let me put the ring on."

"Jason, it's not just me. If it were I'd leave with you this instant. We'd go to Hong Kong,

Siberia, Peking. Anywhere. But it's not just me; I have to stay."

"It's not just you," he repeated. He took the ring and tossed the box aside. "And *I* have to stay. Do you think I'd leave you again? Do you think I could leave what's upstairs or the chance to have more that I can watch grow up? I'm not going anywhere."

"But you said—Hong Kong."

"I quit." When he grinned he felt the pressure of years melt away. "Today. That was one of the things I took care of this afternoon. I'm going to write a book." He took her by the shoulders. "I'm out of a job, I'm living in a room at the inn and asking you to marry me."

The breath backed up in her lungs. Her heart was pounding. Yes, she'd always believed in magic. It was standing in front of her. "Ten years ago, I thought I loved you as much as it was possible to love. You were a boy. In the last few days I've learned that loving a man is something quite different." She paused and saw the ring in his hand explode with the joyful lights on the tree. "If you'd asked me ten years ago I'd have said yes."

"Faith—"

With a laugh, she threw her arms around his neck. "You're going to get the same answer now. Oh, I love you, Jason, more than ever."

"We've got years to make up for."

"Yes." She met his mouth with equal hunger, equal hope. "We will. The three of us."

"The three of us." He let his forehead rest against hers. "I want more."

"We've more than enough time to give Clara a baby brother or sister for next Christmas." Her lips sought his again. "We've got more than enough time for everything."

They both heard the bells peal out from the town hall. Midnight.

"Merry Christmas, Faith."

She felt the ring slide onto her finger. All wishes were granted. "Welcome home, Jason."

* * * * *

ALL I WANT FOR CHRISTMAS

Prologue

Zeke and Zack huddled in the tree house. Important business, any plots or plans, and all punishments for infractions of the rules, were discussed in the sturdy wooden hideaway tucked in the branches of the dignified old sycamore.

Today, a light rain tapped on the tin roof and dampened the dark green leaves. It was still warm enough in the first days of September that the boys wore T-shirts. Red for Zeke, blue for Zack.

They were twins, as identical as the sides of a two-headed coin. Their father had used the color code since their birth to avoid confusion.

When they switched colors—as they often did—they could fool anyone in Taylor's Grove. Except their father.

He was on their minds at the moment. They had already discussed, at length, the anticipated delights and terrors of their first day in real school. The first day in first grade.

They would ride the bus, as they had done the year before, in kindergarten. But this time they would stay in Taylor's Grove Elementary for a full day, just like the big kids. Their cousin Kim had told them that *real* school wasn't a playground.

Zack, the more introspective of the two, had thought over, worried about and dissected this problem for weeks. There were terrible, daunting terms like *homework* and *class participation*, that Kim tossed around. They knew that she, a sophomore in high school, was often loaded down with books. Big, thick books with no pictures.

And sometimes, when she was baby-sitting for them, she had her nose stuck in them for hours. For as long a time as she would have the telephone stuck to her ear, and that was long.

It was pretty scary stuff for Zack, the champion worrier.

Their father would help them, of course. This was something Zeke, the eternal optimist, had pointed out. Didn't they both know how to read stuff like *Green Eggs and Ham* and *The Cat in the Hat* because their dad helped them sound out the words? And they both knew how to write the whole alphabet, and their names and short things, because he showed them.

The trouble was, he had to work and take care of the house and them, as well as Commander Zark, the big yellow dog they'd saved from the animal shelter two years before. Their dad had, as Zack pointed out, an awful lot to do. And now that they were going to go to school, and have assignments and projects and real report cards, he was going to need help.

"He's got Mrs. Hollis to come in once a week and do stuff." Zeke ran his miniature Corvette around the imaginary racetrack on the tree-house floor.

"It's not enough." A frown puckered Zack's

forehead and clouded his lake blue eyes. He exhaled with a long-suffering sigh, ruffling the dark hair that fell over his forehead. "He needs the companionship of a good woman, and we need a mother's love. I heard Mrs. Hollis say so to Mr. Perkins at the post office."

"He hangs around with Aunt Mira sometimes. She's a good woman."

"But she doesn't live with us. And she doesn't have time to help us with science projects." Science projects were a particular terror for Zack. "We need to find a mom." When Zeke only snorted, Zack narrowed his eyes. "We're going to have to spell in first grade."

Zeke caught his lower lip between his teeth. Spelling was his personal nightmare. "How're we going to find one?"

Now Zack smiled. He had, in his slow, careful way, figured it all out. "We're going to ask Santa Claus."

"He doesn't bring moms," Zeke said with the deep disdain that can only be felt by one sibling for another. "He brings toys and stuff. And it's forever until Christmas, anyway."

"No, it's not. Mrs. Hollis was bragging to Mr. Perkins how she already had half her Christmas shopping done. She said how looking ahead meant you could enjoy the holiday."

"Everybody enjoys Christmas. It's the best."

"Uh-uh. Lots of people get mad. Remember how we went to the mall last year with Aunt Mira and she complained and complained about the crowds and the prices and how there weren't any parking spaces?"

Zeke merely shrugged. He didn't look back as often, or as clearly, as his twin, but he took Zack at his word. "I guess."

"So, if we ask now, Santa'll have plenty of time to find the right mom."

"I still say he doesn't bring moms."

"Why not? If we really need one, and we don't ask for too much else?"

"We were going to ask for two-wheelers," Zeke reminded him.

"We could still ask for them," Zack decided. "But not a bunch of other things. Just a mom and the bikes."

It was Zeke's turn to sigh. He didn't care for the idea of giving up his big, long list. But the idea of a mother was beginning to appeal. They'd never had one, and the mystery of it attracted. "So what kind do we ask for?"

"We got to write it down."

Zack took a notebook and a stubby pencil from the table pushed against the wall. They sat on the floor and, with much argument and discussion, composed.

Dear Santa,
We have been good.

Zeke wanted to put in very good, but Zack, the conscience, rejected the idea.

We feed Zark and help Dad. We want a mom for Crissmas. A nice one who smells good and is not meen. She can smile a lot and have yello hair. She has to like little boys and big dogs. She wont mind dirt and bakes cookys. We want a pretty one who is smart and helps us with home-work. We will take good care of her. We want biks a red one and a bloo one. You have lots of time to find the mom and make the biks so you can enjoi the hollidays. Thank you. Love, Zeke and Zack.

Chapter 1

Taylor's Grove, population two thousand three hundred and forty. No, forty-one, Nell thought smugly, as she strolled into the high school auditorium. She'd only been in town for two months, but already she was feeling territorial. She loved the slow pace, the tidy yards and little shops. She loved the easy gossip of neighbors, the front-porch swings, the frost-heaved sidewalks.

If anyone had told her, even a year before, that she would be trading in Manhattan for a dot on the map in western Maryland, she would have thought them mad. But here she was, Taylor's Grove High's new music teacher, as snug and settled in as an old hound in front of a fire.

She'd needed the change, that was certain. In the past year she'd lost her roommate to marriage and inherited a staggering rent she simply wasn't able to manage on her own. The replacement roommate, whom Nell had carefully interviewed, had moved out, as well. Taking everything of value out of the apartment. That nasty little adventure had led to the final, even nastier showdown with her almost-fiancé. When Bob berated her, called her stupid, naive and careless, Nell had decided it was time to cut her losses.

She'd hardly given Bob his walking papers when she received her own. The school where she had taught for three years was downsizing, as they had euphemistically put it. The position of music teacher had been eliminated, and so had Nell.

An apartment she could no longer afford, all but empty, a fiancé who had considered her optimistic nature a liability and the prospect of the unemployment line had taken the sheen off New York.

Once Nell decided to move, she'd decided to move big. The idea of teaching in a small town had sprung up fully rooted. An inspiration, she thought now, for she already felt as if she'd lived here for years.

Her rent was low enough that she could live alone and like it. Her apartment, the entire top floor of a remodeled old house, was a short, enjoyable walk from a campus that included elementary, middle and high schools.

Only two weeks after that first nervous day of school, she was feeling proprietary about her students and was looking forward to her first after-school session with her chorus.

She was determined to create a holiday program that would knock the town's socks off.

The battered piano was center stage. She walked to it and sat. Her students would be filing in shortly, but she had a moment.

She limbered up her mind and her fingers with the blues, an old Muddy Waters tune. Old, scarred pianos were meant to play the blues, she thought, and enjoyed herself.

"Man, she's so cool," Holly Linstrom murmured to Kim as they slipped into the rear of the auditorium.

"Yeah." Kim had a hand on the shoulder of each of her twin cousins, a firm grip that ordered quiet and promised reprisals. "Old Mr. Striker never played anything like that."

"And her clothes are so, like, now." Admiration and envy mixed as Holly scanned the pipe-stem pants, long overshirt and short striped vest Nell wore. "I don't know why anybody from New York would come here. Did you see her earrings today? I bet she got them at some hot place on Fifth Avenue."

Nell's jewelry had already become legendary among the female students. She wore the unique and the unusual. Her taste in clothes, her dark gold hair, which fell just short of her shoulders and always seemed miraculously and expertly tousled, her quick, throaty laugh and her lack of formality had already gone a long way toward endearing her to her students.

"She's got style, all right." But, just then, Kim was more intrigued by the music than by the musician's wardrobe. "Man, I wish I could play like that."

"Man, I wish I could look like that," Holly returned, and giggled.

Sensing an audience, Nell glanced back and grinned. "Come on in, girls. Free concert."

"It sounds great, Miss Davis." With her grip firm on her two charges, Kim started down the sloping aisle toward the stage. "What is it?"

"Muddy Waters. We'll have to shoehorn a little blues education into the curriculum." Sitting back, she studied the two sweet-faced boys on either side of Kim. There was a quick, odd surge of recognition that she didn't understand. "Well, hi, guys."

When they smiled back, identical dimples popped out on the left side of their mouths. "Can you play 'Chopsticks'?" Zeke wanted to know.

Before Kim could express her humiliation at the question, Nell spun into a rousing rendition.

"How's that?" she asked when she'd finished.

"That's neat."

"I'm sorry, Miss Davis. I'm kind of stuck with them for an hour. They're my cousins. Zeke and Zack Taylor."

"The Taylors of Taylor's Grove." Nell swiveled away from the piano. "I bet you're brothers. I see a slight family resemblance."

Both boys grinned and giggled. "We're twins," Zack informed her.

"Really? Now I bet I'm supposed to guess who's who." She came to the edge of the stage, sat and eyed the boys narrowly. They grinned back. Each had recently lost a left front tooth. "Zeke," she said, pointing a finger. "And Zack."

Pleased and impressed, they nodded. "How'd you know?"

It was pointless, and hardly fun, to mention that she'd had a fifty-fifty shot. "Magic. Do you guys like to sing?"

"Sort of. A little."

"Well, today you can listen. You can sit right in the front row and be our test audience."

"Thanks, Miss Davis," Kim murmured, and gave the boys a friendly shove toward the seats. "They're pretty good most of the time. Stay," she ordered, with an older cousin's absolute authority.

Nell winked at the boys as she stood, then gestured to the other students filing in. "Come on up. Let's get started."

* * *

A lot of the business onstage seemed boring to the twins. There was just talking at first, and confusion as sheet music was passed out and boys and girls were assigned positions.

But Zack was watching Nell. She had pretty hair and nice big brown eyes. Like Zark's, he thought with deep affection. Her voice was kind of funny, sort of scratchy and deep, but nice. Now and again she looked back toward him and smiled. When she did, his heart acted strange, kind of beating hard, like he'd been running.

She turned to a group of girls and sang. It was a Christmas song, which made Zack's eyes widen. He wasn't sure of the name, something about a midnight clear, but he recognized it from the records his dad played around the holiday.

A Christmas song. A Christmas wish.

"It's her." He hissed it to his brother, rapping Zeke hard in the ribs.

"Who?"

"It's the mom."

Zeke stopped playing with the action figure

he'd had stuck in his pocket and looked up onstage, where Nell was now directing the alto section. "Kim's teacher is the mom?"

"She has to be." Deadly excited, Zeke kept his voice in a conspiratorial whisper. "Santa's had enough time to get the letter. She was singing a Christmas song, and she's got yellow hair and a nice smile. She likes little boys, too. I can tell."

"Maybe." Not quite convinced, Zeke studied Nell. She was pretty, he thought. And she laughed a lot, even when some of the big kids made mistakes. But that didn't mean she liked dogs or baked cookies. "We can't know for sure yet."

Zack huffed out an impatient breath. "She knew us. She knew which was which. Magic." His eyes were solemn as he looked at his brother. "It's the mom."

"Magic," Zeke repeated, and stared, goggle-eyed, at Nell. "Do we have to wait till Christmas to get her?"

"I guess so. Probably." That was a puzzle Zack would have to work on.

When Mac Taylor pulled his pickup truck in front of the high school, his mind was on a dozen varied problems. What to fix the kids for dinner. How to deal with the flooring on his Meadow Street project. When to find a couple hours to drive to the mall and pick up new underwear for the boys. The last time he folded laundry, he'd noticed that most of what they had was doomed for the rag pile. He had to deal with a lumber delivery first thing in the morning and a pile of paperwork that night.

And Zeke was nervous about his first spelling test, which was coming up in a few days.

Pocketing his keys, Mac rolled his shoulders. He'd been swinging a hammer for the better part of eight hours. He didn't mind the aches. It was a good kind of fatigue, a kind that meant he'd accomplished something. His renovation of the house on Meadow Street was on schedule and on budget. Once it was done, he would have to decide whether to put it on the market or rent it.

His accountant would try to decide for him, but Mac knew the final choice would remain in his own hands. That was the way he preferred it.

As he strode from the parking lot to the high school, he looked around. His great-great-grandfather had founded the town—hardly more than a village back then, settled along Taylor's Creek and stretching over the rolling hills to Taylor's Meadow.

There'd been no lack of ego in old Macauley Taylor.

But Mac had lived in DC for more than twelve years. It had been six years since he returned to Taylor's Grove, but he hadn't lost his pleasure or his pride in it, the simple appreciation for the hills and the trees and the shadows of mountains in the distance.

He didn't think he ever would.

There was the faintest of chills in the air now, and a good strong breeze from the west. But they had yet to have a frost, and the leaves were still a deep summer green. The good weather made his life easier on a couple of levels. As long as it held, he'd be able to finish the outside work on his project in comfort. And the boys could enjoy the afternoons and evenings in the yard.

There was a quick twinge of guilt as he

pulled open the heavy doors and stepped into the school. His work had kept them stuck inside this afternoon. The coming of fall meant that his sister was diving headfirst into several of her community projects. He couldn't impose on her by asking her to watch the twins. Kim's after-school schedule was filling up, and he simply couldn't accept the idea of having his children becoming latchkey kids.

Still, the solution had suited everyone. Kim would take the kids to her rehearsals, and he would save his sister a trip to school by picking them all up and driving them home.

Kim would have a driver's license in a few more months. A fact she was reminding everyone about constantly. But he doubted he'd plunk his boys down in the car with his sixteen-year-old niece at the wheel, no matter how much he loved and trusted her.

You coddle them. Mac rolled his eyes as his sister's voice played in his head. *You can't always be mother and father to them, Mac. If you're not interested in finding a wife, then you'll have to learn to let go a little.*

Like hell he would, Mac thought.

As he neared the auditorium, he heard the sound of young voices raised in song. Subtle harmony. A good, emotional sound that made him smile even before he recognized the tune. A Christmas hymn. It was odd to hear it now, with the sweat from his day just drying on his back.

He pulled open the auditorium doors, and was flooded with it. Charmed, he stood at the back and looked out on the singers. One of the students played the piano. A pretty little thing, Mac mused, who looked up now and then, gesturing, as if to urge her classmates to give more.

He wondered where the music teacher was, then spotted his boys sitting in the front row. He walked quietly down the aisle, raising a hand when he saw Kim's eyes shift to his. He settled behind the boys and leaned forward.

"Pretty good show, huh?"

"Dad!" Zack nearly squealed, then remembered just in time to speak in a hissing whisper. "It's Christmas."

"Sure sounds like it. How's Kim doing?"

"She's real good." Zeke now considered

himself an expert on choral arrangements. "She's going to have a solo."

"No kidding?"

"She got red in the face when Miss Davis asked her to sing by herself, but she did okay." Zeke was much more interested in Nell right then. "She's pretty, isn't she?"

A little amazed at this announcement—the twins were fond of Kim, but rarely complimentary—he nodded. "Yeah. The prettiest girl in school."

"We could have her over for dinner sometime," Zack said slyly. "Couldn't we?"

Baffled now, Mac ruffled his son's hair. "You know Kim can come over whenever she wants."

"Not her." In a gesture that mimicked his father, Zack rolled his eyes. "Jeez, Dad. Miss Davis."

"Who's Miss Davis?"

"The m—" Zeke's announcement was cut off by his twin's elbow.

"The teacher," Zack finished with a snarling look at his brother. "The pretty one." He pointed, and his father followed the direction to the piano.

"She's the teacher?" Before Mac could reevaluate, the music flowed to a stop and Nell rose.

"That was great, really. A very solid first run-through." She pushed her tousled hair back. "But we need a lot of work. I'd like to schedule the next rehearsal for Monday after school. Three forty-five."

There was already a great deal of movement and mumbling, so Nell pitched her voice to carry the rest of her instructions over the noise. Satisfied, she turned to smile at the twins and found herself grinning at an older, and much more disturbing version, of the Taylor twins.

No doubt he was the father, Nell thought. The same thick dark hair curled down over the collar of a grimy T-shirt. The same lake-water eyes framed in long, dark lashes stared back at her. His face might lack the soft, slightly rounded appeal of his sons', but the more rugged version was just as attractive. He was long, rangy, with the kind of arms that looked tough without being obviously muscled. He was tanned and more than a little dirty. She wondered if he had a dimple at the left corner of his mouth when he smiled.

"Mr. Taylor." Rather than bother with the stairs, she hopped off the stage, as agile as any of her students. She held out a hand decorated with rings.

"Miss Davis." He covered her hand with his callused one, remembering too late that it was far from clean. "I appreciate you letting the kids hang out while Kim rehearsed."

"No problem. I work better with an audience." Tilting her head, she looked down at the twins. "Well, guys, how'd we do?"

"It was really neat." This from Zeke. "We like Christmas songs the best."

"Me too."

Still flustered and flattered by the idea of having a solo, Kim joined them. "Hi, Uncle Mac. I guess you met Miss Davis."

"Yeah." There wasn't much more to say. He still thought she looked too young to be a teacher. Not the teenager he'd taken her for, he realized. But that creamy, flawless skin and that tidy little frame were deceiving. And very attractive.

"Your niece is very talented." In a natural movement, Nell wrapped an arm around Kim's shoulders. "She has a wonderful voice and a quick understanding of what the music means. I'm delighted to have her."

"We like her, too," Mac said as Kim flushed.

Zack shifted from foot to foot. They weren't supposed to be talking about dumb old Kim. "Maybe you could come visit us sometime, Miss Davis," he piped up. "We live in the big brown house out on Mountain View Road."

"That'd be nice." But Nell noted that Zack's father didn't second the invitation, or look particularly pleased by it. "And you guys are welcome to be our audience anytime. You work on that solo, Kim."

"I will, Miss Davis. Thanks."

"Nice to have met you, Mr. Taylor." As he mumbled a response, Nell hopped back onstage to gather her sheet music.

It was too bad, she thought, that the father lacked the outgoing charm and friendliness of his sons.

Chapter 2

It didn't get much better than a drive in the country on a balmy fall afternoon. Nell remembered how she used to spend a free Saturday in New York. A little shopping—she supposed if she missed anything about Manhattan, it was the shopping—maybe a walk in the park. Never a jog. Nell didn't believe in running if walking would get you to the same place.

And driving, well, that was even better. She hadn't realized what a pleasure it was to not only own a car but be able to zip it along winding country roads with the windows open and the radio blaring.

The leaves were beginning to turn now as September hit its stride. Blushes of color competed with the green. On one particular road that she turned down out of impulse, the big trees arched over the asphalt, a spectacular canopy that let light flicker and flit through as the road followed the snaking trail of a rushing creek.

It wasn't until she glanced up at a road sign that she realized she was on Mountain View.

The big brown house, Zack had said, she remembered. There weren't a lot of houses here, two miles outside of town, but she caught glimpses of some through the shading trees. Brown ones, white ones, blue ones—some close to the creek bed, others high atop narrow, pitted lanes that served as driveways.

A lovely place to live, she thought. And to raise children. However taciturn and stiff Mac Taylor might have been, he'd done a wonderful job with his sons.

She already knew he'd done the job alone. It hadn't taken long for Nell to understand the rhythm of small towns. A comment here, a casual question there, and she'd had what amounted to a full biography of the Taylor men.

Mac had lived in Washington, DC, since his family moved out of town when he was a young teenager. Six years ago, twin infants in tow, he'd moved back. His older sister had gone to a local college and married a town boy and settled in Taylor's Grove years before. It was she, the consensus was, who had urged him to come back and raise his children there when his wife took off.

Left the poor little infants high and dry, Mrs. Hollis had told Nell over the bread rack at the general store. Run off with barely a word, and hadn't said a peep since. And young Macauley Taylor had been mother and father both to his twins ever since.

Maybe, Nell thought cynically, just maybe, if he'd actually talked to his wife now and again, she'd have stayed with him.

Not fair, she thought. There was no decent excuse she could think of for a mother deserting her infant children, then not contacting them for six years. Whatever kind of husband Mac Taylor had been, the children deserved better.

She thought of them now, those impish mirror images. She'd always been fond of children, and the Taylor twins were a double dose of enjoyment. She'd gotten quite a kick out of having them in the audience once or twice a week during rehearsals. Zeke had even shown her his very first spelling test—with its big silver star. If he hadn't missed just one word, he'd told her, he'd have gotten a gold one.

Nor had she missed the shy looks Zack sent her, or the quick smiles before he flushed and lowered his eyes. It was very sweet to be responsible for his first case of puppy love.

She sighed with pleasure as the car burst out from under the canopy of trees and into the light. Here were the mountains that gave the road its name, streaking suddenly into the vivid blue sky. The road curved and snaked, but they were always there, dark, distant and dramatic.

The land rose on either side of the road, in rolling hills and rocky outcroppings. She slowed when she spotted a house on the crest of a hill. Brown. Probably cedar, she thought, with a stone foundation and what seemed like acres of sparkling glass. There was a deck stretched across the second story, and there were trees that shaded and sheltered. A tire swing hung from one.

She wondered if this was indeed the Taylor house. She hoped her new little friends lived in such a solid, well-planned home. Then she passed the mailbox planted at the side of the road just at the edge of the long lane.

M. Taylor and sons.

It made her smile. Pleased, she punched the gas pedal and was baffled when the car bucked and stuttered.

"What's the problem here?" she muttered, easing off on the pedal and punching it again. This time the car shuddered and stopped dead. "For heaven's sake." Only mildly annoyed, she started to turn the key to start it again, and glanced at the dash. The little gas pump beside the gauge was brightly lit.

"Stupid," she said aloud, berating herself. "Stupid, stupid. Weren't you supposed to get gas *before* you left town?" She sat back, sighed. She'd meant to, really. Just as she'd meant to stop and fill up the day before, right after class.

Now she was two miles out of town without even fumes to ride on. Blowing the hair out of her eyes, she looked out at the home of M. Taylor and sons. A quarter-mile hike, she estimated. Which made it a lot better than two miles. And she had, more or less, been invited.

She grabbed her keys and started up the lane.

She was no more than halfway when the boys spotted her. They came racing down the rocky, pitted lane at a speed that stopped her heart. Surefooted as young goats, they streaked toward her. Coming up behind was a huge yellow dog.

"Miss Davis! Hi, Miss Davis! Did you come to see us?"

"Sort of." Laughing, she crouched down to give them both a hug and caught the faint scent of chocolate. Before she could comment, the dog decided he wanted in on the action. He was restrained enough to plant his huge paws on her thighs, rather than her shoulders.

Zack held his breath, then let it out when she chuckled and bent down to rub Zark on head and shoulders. "You're a big one, aren't you? A big beauty."

Zark lapped her hand in perfect agreement. Nell caught a look exchanged quickly between the twins. One that seemed both smug and excited.

"You like dogs?" Zeke asked.

"Sure I do. Maybe I'll get one now. I never had the heart to lock one up in a New York apartment." She only laughed again when Zark sat and politely lifted a paw. "Too late for formalities now, buddy," she told him, but shook it anyway. "I was out driving, and I ran out of gas right smack at the bottom of your lane. Isn't that funny?"

Zack's grin nearly split his face. She liked dogs. She'd stopped right at their house. It was more magic, he was sure of it. "Dad'll fix it. He can fix anything." Confident now that he had her on his own ground, Zack took her hand. Not to be outdone, Zeke clasped the other.

"Dad's out back in the shop, building a 'rondak chair."

"A rocking chair?" Nell suggested.

"Nuh-uh. A 'rondak chair. Come see."

They hauled her around the house, passed

a curving sunroom that caught the southern light. There was another deck in the back, with steps leading down to a flagstone patio. The shop in the backyard—the same cedar as the house—looked big enough to hold a family of four. Nell heard the thwack of a hammer on wood.

Bursting with excitement, Zeke raced through the shop door. "Dad! Dad! Guess what?"

"I guess you've taken another five years off my life."

Nell heard Mac's voice, deep and amused and tolerant, and found herself hesitating. "I hate to bother him when he's busy," she said to Zeke. "Maybe I can just call the station in town."

"It's okay, come on." Zack dragged her a few more feet into the doorway.

"See?" Zeke said importantly. "She came!"

"Yeah, I see." Caught off-balance by the unexpected visit, Mac set his hammer down on his workbench. He pushed up the brim of his cap and frowned without really meaning to. "Miss Davis."

"I'm sorry to bother you, Mr. Taylor," she began, then saw the project he was working on. "An Adirondack chair," she murmured, and grinned. "A 'rondak chair. It's nice."

"Will be." Was he supposed to offer her coffee? he wondered. A tour of the house? What? She shouldn't be pretty, he thought irrelevantly. There was nothing particularly striking about her. Well, maybe the eyes. They were so big and brown. But the rest really was ordinary. It must be the way it was put together, he decided, that made it extraordinary.

Not certain whether she was amused or uncomfortable at the way he was staring at her, Nell launched into her explanation. "I was out driving. Partly for the pleasure of it, and partly to try to familiarize myself with the area. I've only lived here a couple months."

"Is that right?"

"Miss Davis is from New York City, Dad," Zack reminded him. "Kim told you."

"Yeah, she did." He picked up his hammer again, set it down. "Nice day for a drive."

"I thought so. So nice I forgot to get gas before I left town. I ran out at the bottom of your lane."

A flicker of suspicion darkened his eyes. "That's handy."

"Not especially." Her voice, though still friendly, had cooled. "If I could use your phone to call the station in town, I'd appreciate it."

"I've got gas," he muttered.

"See, I told you Dad could fix it," Zack said proudly. "We've got brownies," he added, struggling madly for a way to get her to stay longer. "Dad made them. You can have one."

"I thought I smelled chocolate." She scooped Zack up and sniffed at his face. "I've got a real nose for it."

Moving on instinct, Mac plucked Zack out of her arms. "You guys go get some brownies. We'll get the gas."

"Okay!" They raced off together.

"I wasn't going to abduct him, Mr. Taylor."

"Didn't say you were." He walked to the doorway, glanced back. "The gas is in the shed."

Lips pursed, she followed him out. "Were you traumatized by a teacher at an impressionable age, Mr. Taylor?"

"Mac. Just Mac. No, why?"

"I wondered if we have a personal or a professional problem here."

"I don't have a problem." He stopped at the small shed where he kept his lawn mower and garden tools, then said, "Funny how the kids told you where we lived, and you ran out of gas right here."

She took a long breath, studying him as he bent over to pick up a can, straighten and turn. "Look, I'm no happier about it than you, and after this reception, probably a lot less happy. It happens that this is the first car I've ever owned, and I'm still a little rough on the finer points. I ran out of gas last month in front of the general store. You're welcome to check."

He shrugged, feeling stupid and unnecessarily prickly. "Sorry."

"Forget it. If you'll give me the can, I'll use what I need to get back to town, then I'll have it filled and returned."

"I'll take care of it," he muttered.

"I don't want to put you out." She reached for the can and that started a quick tug-of-war. After a moment, the dimple at the corner of his mouth winked.

"I'm bigger than you."

She stepped back and blew the hair out of her eyes. "Fine. Go be a man, then." Scowling, she followed him around the house, then tried to fight off her foul mood as the twins came racing up. They each held a paper towel loaded with brownies.

"Dad makes the best brownies in the whole world," Zack told her, holding up his offering.

Nell took one and bit in. "You may be right," she was forced to admit, her mouth full. "And I know my brownies."

"Can you make cookies?" Zeke wanted to know.

"I happened to be known far and wide for my chocolate-chip." Her smile became puzzled as the boys eyed each other and nodded. "You come visit me sometime, and we'll whip some up."

"Where do you live?" Since his father wasn't paying close attention, Zeke stuffed an entire brownie in his mouth.

"On Market Street, right off the square.

The old brick house with the three porches. I rent the top floor."

"Dad owns that," Zack told her. "He bought it and fixed it all up and now he rents it out. We're in real estate."

"Oh." She let out a long breath. "Really." Her rent checks were mailed to Taylor Management...on Mountain View Road.

"So you live in our house," Zack finished up.

"In a manner of speaking."

"The place okay with you?" Mac asked.

"Yes, it's fine. I'm very comfortable there. It's convenient to school."

"Dad buys houses and fixes them up all the time." Zeke wondered if he could get away with another brownie. "He likes to fix stuff."

It was obvious from the tidy and thoughtful renovation of the old house she now lived in that their father fixed them very well. "You're a carpenter, then?" she asked, reluctantly addressing Mac.

"Sometimes." They'd reached her car. Mac merely jerked his thumb to signal the boys and dog to keep off the road. He unscrewed the gas cap and spoke without looking around. "If you eat another one of those, Zeke, I'm going to have to have your stomach pumped."

Sheepishly Zeke replaced the brownie on the paper towel.

"Excellent radar," Nell commented, leaning on the car as Mac added the gas.

"Goes with the territory." He looked at her then. Her hair was windblown and gilded by the sun. Her face was rosy from the walk and the breeze. He didn't like what looking at her did to his pulse rate. "Why Taylor's Grove? It's a long way from New York."

"That's why. I wanted a change." She breathed deep as she looked around, at rock and tree and hill. "I got one."

"Pretty slow, compared to what you'd be used to."

"Slow's something I do very well."

He only shrugged. He suspected she'd be bored senseless in six months and heading out. "Kim's pretty excited about your class. She talks about it almost as much as she does getting her driver's license."

"That's quite a compliment. It's a good

school. Not all of my students are as cooperative as Kim, but I like a challenge. I'm going to recommend her for all-state."

Mac tipped the can farther up. "She's really that good?"

"You sound surprised."

He shrugged again. "She always sounded good to me, but the old music teacher never singled her out."

"Rumor is he never took much interest in any of his students individually, or in extra work."

"You got that right. Striker was an old—" He caught himself, glanced back at his kids, who were standing close by, all ears. "He was old," Mac repeated. "And set in his ways. Always the same Christmas program, the same spring program."

"Yes, I've looked over his class notes. I'd say everyone should be in for a surprise this year. I'm told no student from Taylor's Grove ever went to all-state."

"Not that I heard."

"Well, we're going to change that." Satisfied now that they had managed a reasonable conversation, she tossed back her hair. "Do you sing?"

"In the shower." His dimple flickered again as his sons giggled. "No comments from the brats."

"He sings really, really loud," Zeke said, without fear of reprisal. "And he gets Zark howling."

"I'm sure that would be quite a show." Nell scratched the grinning dog between the ears. He thumped his tail, and then some internal clock struck and had him pivoting and racing up the hill.

"Here you go, Miss Davis. Here." Both boys stuffed the loaded paper towels into her hands and barreled off after the dog.

"I guess they don't keep still very long," she murmured, watching them chase the dog up the rise.

"That was nearly a record. They like you."

"I'm a likable person." She smiled, glancing back at him, only to find him staring at her again with that not-quite-pleased look in his eyes. "At least in most cases. If you'd just put that on the back seat, I'll have it filled up for you."

"It's not a problem." Mac replaced her gas cap and kept the empty can. "We're friendly in Taylor's Grove. In most cases."

"Let me know when I'm off probation." She leaned into her car to set the brownies on the passenger seat. Mac had a tantalizing and uncomfortable view of her jean-clad bottom. He could smell her, too, something light and spicy that spun in his head a lot more potently than the gas fumes.

"I didn't mean it like that."

Her head popped back out of the car. She licked a smear of brownie from her finger as she straightened. "Maybe not. In any case, I appreciate the help." Her grin flashed as she opened the car door. "And the chocolate."

"Anytime," he heard himself say, and wanted to regret it.

She settled behind the steering wheel, tossed him a quick, saucy smile. "Like hell." Then she laughed and turned the ignition, revving the engine in a way that made Mac wince. "You should drop in on rehearsals now and again, Mac, instead of waiting out in the parking lot. You might learn something."

He wasn't certain he wanted to. "Put on your seat belt," he ordered.

"Oh, yeah." Obligingly, she buckled up. "Just not used to it yet. Say bye to the twins." She zoomed off at a speed just this side of reckless, waving a careless and glittering hand out the window.

Mac watched her until she rounded the bend, then slowly rubbed his stomach where the muscles were knotted. Something about that woman, he thought. Something about the way she was put together made him feel like he was defrosting after a very long freeze.

Chapter 3

Another half hour, Mac figured, and he could finish taping the drywall in the master bedroom. Maybe get the first coat of mud on. He glanced at his watch, calculated that the kids were home from school. But it was Mrs. Hollis's day, and she'd stay until five. That would give him plenty of time to hit the drywall, clean up and get home.

Maybe he'd give himself and the kids a treat and pick up pizza.

He'd learned not to mind cooking, but he still resented the time it took—the thinking, the preparation, the cleaning up afterward. Six years as a single parent had given him a whole new perspective on how hard his mother—that rare and old-fashioned homemaker—had worked.

Pausing a moment, he took a look around the master suite. He'd taken walls out, built others, replaced the old single-pane windows with double glazed. Twin skylights let in the fading sunlight of early October.

Now there were three spacious bedrooms on the second floor of the old house, rather than the four choppy rooms and oversize hallway he'd started with. The master suite would boast a bathroom large enough for tub and separate shower stall. He was toying with using glass block for that. He'd been wanting to work with it for some time.

If he stayed on schedule, the place would be put together by Christmas, and on the sale or rental market by the first of the year.

He really should sell it, Mac thought, running a hand over the drywall he'd nailed up that afternoon. He had to get over this sense of possession whenever he worked on a house.

In the blood, he supposed. His father had

made a good living buying up damaged or de-
pressed property, rehabing and renting. Mac
had discovered just how satisfying it was to
own something you'd made fine with your
own hands.

Like the old brick house Nell lived in now.
He wondered if she knew it was more than a
hundred and fifty years old, that she was living
in a piece of history.

He wondered if she'd run out of gas again.

He wondered quite a bit about Nell Davis.

And he shouldn't, Mac reminded himself,
and turned away for his tools and tape.
Women were trouble. One way or the other,
they were trouble. One look at Nell and a
smart man could see she was no exception.

He hadn't taken her up on her suggestion
that he drop by the auditorium and catch part
of a rehearsal. He'd started to a couple of
times, but good sense had stopped him. She
was the first woman in a very, very long time
who had stirred him up. He didn't want to be
stirred up, Mac thought with a scowl as he
taped a seam. Couldn't afford to be, he reminded himself. He had too many obligations,

too little free time, and, most important, two sons who were the focus of his life.

Daydreaming about a woman was bad enough. It made a man sloppy in his work, forgetful and…itchy. But doing something about it was worse. Doing something meant you had to find conversation and ways to entertain. A woman expected to be taken places, and pampered. And once you started to fall for her—really fall for her—she had the power to cut out your heart.

Mac wasn't willing to risk his heart again, and he certainly wasn't willing to risk his sons.

He didn't subscribe to that nonsense about children needing a woman's touch, a mother's love. The twins' mother had felt less connection with the children she'd borne than a cat felt toward a litter of kittens. Being female didn't give you a leg up on maternal feelings. It meant you were physically able to carry a child inside you, but it didn't mean that you'd care once that child was in your arms.

Mac stopped taping and swore. He hadn't thought about Angie in years. Not deeply. When he did, he realized the spot was still sore, like an old wound that had healed poorly. That was what he got, he supposed, for letting some little blonde stir him up.

Annoyed with himself, he stripped the last piece of tape off the roll. He needed to concentrate on his work, not on a woman. Determined to finish what he'd started, he marched down the stairs. He had more drywall tape in his truck.

The light outside was softening with the approach of dusk. Shorter days, he thought. Less time.

He was down the steps and onto the walk before he saw her. She was standing just at the edge of the yard, looking up at the house, smiling a little. She wore a suede jacket in a deep burnished orange over faded jeans. Some glittery stones dangled from her ears. Over her shoulder hung a soft-sided briefcase that looked well used.

"Oh. Hi." Surprise lit her eyes when she glanced over, and that immediately made him suspicious. "Is this one of your places?"

"That's right." He moved past her toward the truck and wished he'd held his breath. That scent she wore was subtle and sneaky.

"I was just admiring it. Beautiful stone-work. It looks so sturdy and safe, tucked in with all the trees." She took a deep breath. There was the slap of fall in the air. "It's going to be a beautiful night."

"I guess." He found his tape, then stood, running the roll around in his hands. "Did you run out of gas again?"

"No." She laughed, obviously amused at herself. "I like walking around town this time of day. As a matter of fact, I was heading down to your sister's. She's a few doors down, right?"

His eyes narrowed. He didn't like the idea of the woman he was spending too much time thinking about hanging out with his sister. "Yeah, that's right. Why?"

"Why?" Her attention had been focused on his hands. There was something about them. Hard, callused. Big. She felt a quick and very pleasant flutter in the pit of her stomach. "Why what?"

"Why are you going to Mira's?"

"Oh. I have some sheet music I thought Kim would like."

"Is that right?" He leaned on the truck, measuring her. Her smile was entirely too friendly, he decided. Entirely too attractive. "Is it part of your job description to make house calls with sheet music?"

"It's part of the fun." Her hair ruffled in the light breeze. She scooped it back. "No job's worth the effort or the headaches if you don't have some fun." She looked back at the house. "You have fun, don't you? Taking something and making it yours?"

He started to say something snide, then realized she'd put her finger right on the heart of it. "Yeah. It doesn't always seem like fun when you're tearing out ceilings and having insulation raining down on your head." He smiled a little. "But it is."

"Are you going to let me see?" She tilted her head. "Or are you like a temperamental artist, not willing to show his work until the final brush stroke?"

"There's not much to see." Then he shrugged. "Sure, you can come in if you want."

"Thanks." She started up the walk, glanced

over her shoulder when he stayed by the truck.
"Aren't you going to give me a tour?"

He moved his shoulders again, and joined
her.

"Did you do the trim on my apartment?"

"Yeah."

"It's beautiful work. Looks like cherry."

He frowned, surprised. "It is cherry."

"I like the rounded edges. They soften everything. Do you get a decorator in for the
colors or pick them out yourself?"

"I pick them." He opened the door for her.
"Is there a problem?"

"No. I really love the color scheme in the
kitchen, the slate blue counters, the mauve
floor. Oh, what fabulous stairs." She hurried
across the unfinished living area to the stair-
case.

Mac had worked hard and long on it, tearing out the old and replacing it with dark
chestnut, curving and widening the landing at
the bottom so that it flowed out into the living
space.

It was, undeniably, his current pride
and joy.

"Did you build these?" she murmured, running a hand over the curve of the railing.

"The old ones were broken, dry-rotted. Had to go."

"I have to try them." She dashed up, turning back at the top to grin at him. "No creaks. Good workmanship, but not very sentimental."

"Sentimental?"

"You know, the way you look back on home, how you snuck downstairs as a kid and knew just which steps to avoid because they'd creak and wake up Mom."

All at once he was having trouble with his breathing. "They're chestnut," he said, because he could think of nothing else.

"Whatever, they're beautiful. Whoever lives here has to have kids."

His mouth was dry, unbearably. "Why?"

"Because." On impulse, she planted her butt on the railing and pushed off. Mac's arms came out of their own volition to catch her as she flew off the end. "It was made for sliding," she said breathlessly. She was laughing as she tilted her head up to his.

Something clicked inside her when their eyes met. And the fluttering, not so pleasant this time, came again. Disconcerted, she cleared her throat and searched for something to say.

"You keep popping up," Mac muttered. He had yet to release her, couldn't seem to make his hands obey his head.

"It's a small town."

He only shook his head. His hands were at her waist now, and they seemed determined to slide around and stroke up her back. He thought he felt her tremble—but it might have been him.

"I don't have time for women," he told her, trying to convince himself.

"Well." She tried to swallow, but there was something hard and hot lodged in her throat. "I'm pretty busy myself." She let out a slow breath. Those hands stroking up and down her back were making her weak. "And I'm not really interested. I had a really bad year, as far as relationships go. I think…"

It was very hard to think. His eyes were such a beautiful shade of blue, and so intensely focused on hers. She wasn't sure what he saw, or what he was looking for, but she knew her knees were about to give out.

"I think," she began again, "we'd both be better off if you decide fairly quickly if you're going to kiss me or not. I can't handle this much longer."

Neither could he. Still, he took his time. He was, in all things, a thorough and thoughtful man. His eyes were open and on hers as he lowered his head, as his mouth hovered a breath from hers, as a small, whimpering moan sounded in her throat.

Her vision dimmed as his lips brushed hers. His were soft, firm, terrifyingly patient. The whisper of contact slammed a punch into her stomach. He lingered over her like a gourmet sampling delicacies, deepening the kiss degree by staggering degree until she was clinging to him.

No one had ever kissed her like this. She hadn't known anyone could. Slow and deep and dreamy. The floor seemed to tilt under her feet as he gently sucked her lower lip into his mouth.

She shuddered, groaned, and let herself drown.

She was very potent. The scent and feel and taste of her was overwhelming. He knew he could lose himself here, for a moment, for a lifetime. Her small, tight body was all but plastered to his. Her hands clutched his hair. In contrast to that aggressive gesture, her head fell limply back in a kind of sighing surrender that had his blood bubbling.

He wanted to touch her. His hands were aching with the need to peel off layer after layer and find the pale, smooth skin beneath. To test himself, and her, he slipped his fingers under her sweater, along the soft, hot flesh of her back, while his mouth continued its long, lazy assault on hers.

He imagined laying her down on the floor, on a tarp, on the grass. He imagined watching her face as he pleasured them both, of feeling her arch toward him, open, accepting.

It had been too long, he told himself as his muscles began to coil and his lungs to labor. It had just been too long.

But he didn't believe it. And it frightened him.

Unsteady, he lifted his head, drew back. Even as he began the retreat, she leaned against him, letting her head fall onto his chest. Unable to resist, he combed his fingers through her hair and cradled her there.

"My head's spinning," she murmured. "What was that?"

"It was a kiss, that's all." He needed to believe that. It would help to ease the tightness around his heart and his loins.

"I think I saw stars." Still staggered, she shifted so that she could look up at him. Her lips curved, but her eyes didn't echo the smile. "That's a first for me."

If he didn't do something fast, he was going to kiss her again. He set her firmly on her feet. "It doesn't change anything."

"Was there something to change?"

The light was nearly gone now. It helped that he couldn't see her clearly in the gloom. "I don't have time for women. And I'm just not interested in starting anything."

"Oh." Where had that pain come from? she wondered, and had to fight to keep from rubbing a hand over her heart. "That was quite a kiss, for a disinterested man." Reaching down, she scooped up the briefcase she'd dropped before she'd run up the stairs. "I'll get out of your way. I wouldn't want to waste any more of your valuable time."

"You don't have to get huffy about it."

"Huffy." Her teeth snapped together. She jabbed a finger into his chest. "I'm well beyond huffy, pal, and working my way past steamed. You've got some ego, Mac. What, do you think I came around here to seduce you?"

"I don't know why you came around."

"Well, I won't be around again." She settled her briefcase on her shoulder, jerked her chin up. "Nobody twisted your arm."

He was dealing with an uncomfortable combination of desire and guilt. "Yours, either."

"I'm not the one making excuses. You know, I can't figure out how such an insensitive clod could raise two charming and adorable kids."

"Leave my boys out of this."

The edge to the order had her eyes narrowing to slits. "Oh, so I have designs on them now, too? You idiot!" She stormed for the door, whirling at the last moment for a parting shot. "I hope they don't inherit your warped view of the female species!"

She slammed the door hard enough to have the bad-tempered sound echoing through the house. Mac scowled and jammed his hands in his pockets. He didn't have a warped view, damn it. And his kids were his business.

Chapter 4

Nell stood center stage and lifted her hands. She waited until she was sure every student's eyes were on her, then let it rip.

There was very little that delighted her more than the sound of young voices raised in song. She let the sound fill her, keeping her ears and eyes sharp as she moved around the stage directing. She couldn't hold back the grin. The kids were into this one. Doing Bruce Springsteen and the E Street Band's version of "Santa Claus Is Coming to Town" was a departure from the standard carols and hymns their former choral director had arranged year after year.

She could see their eyes light up as they got into the rhythm. Now punch it, she thought, pulling more from the bass section as they hit the chorus. Have fun with it. Now the soprano section, high and bright... And the altos... Tenors... Bass...

She flashed a smile to signal her approval as the chorus flowered again.

"Good job," she announced. "Tenors, a little more next time. You guys don't want the bass section drowning you out. Holly, you're dropping your chin again. Now we have time for one more run-through of 'I'll Be Home for Christmas.' Kim?"

Kim tried to ignore the little flutter around her heart and the elbow nudge from Holly. She stepped down from her position in the second row and stood in front of the solo mike as though she were facing a firing squad.

"It's okay to smile, you know," Nell told her gently. "And remember your breathing. Sing to the last row, and don't forget to feel the words. Tracy." She held out a finger toward the pianist she'd dragooned from her second-period music class.

The intro started quietly. Using her hands, her face, her eyes, Nell signaled the beginning of the soft, harmonious, background humming. Then Kim began to sing. Too tentatively at first. Nell knew they would have to work on those initial nerves.

But the girl had talent, and emotion. Three bars in, Kim was too caught up in the song to be nervous. She was pacing it well, Nell thought, pleased. Kim had learned quite a bit in the past few weeks about style. The sentimental song suited her, her range, her looks.

Nell brought the chorus in, holding them back. They were background now for Kim's rich, romantic voice. Feeling her own eyes stinging, Nell thought that if they did it this well on the night of the concert, there wouldn't be a dry eye in the house.

"Lovely," Nell said when the last notes had died away. "Really lovely. You guys have come a long way in a very short time. I'm awfully proud of you. Now scram, and have a great weekend."

While Nell moved to the piano to gather up music, the chatter began behind her.

"You sounded really good," Holly told Kim.

"Honest?"

"Honest. Brad thought so, too." Holly shifted her eyes cagily to the school heartthrob, who was shrugging into his school jacket.

"He doesn't even know I'm alive."

"He does now. He was watching you the whole time. I know, because I was watching him." Holly sighed. "If I looked like Miss Davis, *he'd* be watching *me.*"

Kim laughed, but shot a quick glance toward Brad under her lashes. "She's really fabulous. Just the way she talks to us and stuff. Mr. Striker always crabbed."

"Mr. Striker *was* a crab. See you later, huh?"

"Yeah." It was all Kim could manage, because it looked, it really looked, as though Brad were coming toward her. And he *was* looking at her.

"Hi." He flashed a grin, all white teeth, with a crooked incisor that made her heart flop around in her chest. "You did real good."

"Thanks." Her tongue tied itself into knots. This was Brad, she kept thinking. A senior. Captain of the football team. Student council president. All blond hair and green eyes.

"Miss Davis sure is cool, isn't she?"

"Yeah." Say something, she ordered herself. "She's coming to a party at my house tonight. My mom's having some people over."

"Adults only, huh?"

"No, Holly's coming by and a couple other people." Her heart thundered in her ears as she screwed up her courage. "You could drop by if you wanted."

"That'd be cool. What time?"

She managed to close her mouth and swallow. "Oh, about eight," she said, struggling for the casual touch. "I live on—"

"I know where you live." He grinned at her again, and all but stopped her thundering heart. "Hey, you're not going with Chuck anymore, are you?"

"Chuck?" Who was Chuck? "Oh, no. We hung out for a while, but we sort of broke up over the summer."

"Great. See you later."

He strolled off to join a group of boys who were trooping offstage.

"That's a very cute guy," Nell commented from behind Kim.

"Yeah." The word was a sigh. Kim had stars in her eyes.

"Kimmy has a boyfriend," Zeke sang, in the high-pitched, annoying voice that was reserved for addressing younger siblings—or female cousins.

"Shut up, brat."

He only giggled and began to dance around the stage, singsonging the refrain. Nell saw murder shoot into Kim's eyes and created a diversion.

"Well, I guess you guys don't want to practice 'Jingle Bells' today."

"Yes, we do." Zack stopped twirling around the stage with his brother and dashed to the piano. "I know which one it is," he said, attacking Nell's neat pile of sheet music. "I can find it."

"I'll find it," Zeke said, but his brother was already holding the music up triumphantly.

"Good going." Nell settled on the bench with a boy on either side of her. She played a dramatic opening chord that made them both giggle. "Please, music is a serious business. And one, and two, and..."

They actually sang it now, instead of screaming it, as they had the first time she invited them to try. What they lacked in style, they made up for in enthusiasm. In spades.

Even Kim was grinning by the time they'd finished.

"Now you do one, Miss Davis." Zack gave her his soulful look. "Please."

"Your dad's probably waiting."

"Just one."

"Just one," Zeke echoed.

In a few short weeks, it had become impossible for her to resist them. "Just one," Nell agreed, and reached into the now-messy pile of music. "I picked up something you might like at the mall. I bet you've seen *The Little Mermaid.*"

"Lots of times," Zeke boasted. "We've got the tape and everything."

"Then you'll recognize this." She played the opening of "Part of Your World."

Mac hunched his shoulders against the wind as he headed into the school. He was damn sick and tired of waiting out in the parking lot.

He'd seen the other kids filing out more than ten minutes before.

He had things to do, damn it. Especially since he was stuck going over to Mira's for a party.

He hated parties.

He stomped down the hall. And he heard her. Not the words. He couldn't make out the words, because they were muffled by the auditorium doors. But the sound of her voice, rich and deep. A Scotch-and-soda voice, he'd thought more than once. Sensual, seductive. Sexy.

He opened the door. He had to. And the lush flow of it rolled over him.

A kid's song. He recognized it now from the mermaid movie the boys were still crazy about. He told himself no sane man would get tied up in knots when a woman sang a kid's song.

But he wasn't feeling very sane. Hadn't been since he made the enormous mistake of kissing her.

And he knew that if she'd been alone he would have marched right over to the piano and kissed her again.

But she wasn't alone. Kim was standing behind her, and his children flanked her. Now and again she glanced down at them as she sang, and smiled. Zack was leaning toward her, his head tilting in the way it did just before he climbed into your lap.

Something shifted inside him as he watched. Something painful and frightening. And very, very sweet.

Shaken, Mac stuffed his hands into his pockets, curled those hands into fists. It had to stop. Whatever was happening to him had to stop.

He took a long breath when the music ended. He thought—foolishly, he was sure—that there was something magical humming in the instant of silence that followed.

"We're running late," he called out, determined to break the spell.

Four heads turned his way. The twins began to bounce on the bench.

"Dad! Hey, Dad! We can sing 'Jingle Bells' really good! Want to hear us?"

"I can't." He tried to smile, softening the blow, when Zack's lip poked out. "I'm really running late, kids."

"Sorry, Uncle Mac." Kim scooped up her coat. "We kind of lost track."

While Mac shifted uncomfortably, Nell leaned over and murmured something to his sons. Something, Mac noted, that put a smile back on Zack's face and took the mutinous look off Zeke's. Then both of them threw arms around her and kissed her before they raced offstage for their coats.

"Bye, Miss Davis! Bye!"

"Thanks, Miss Davis," Kim added. "See you later."

Nell made a humming sound and rose to straighten her music.

Mac felt the punch of her cold shoulder all the way in the back of the auditorium. "Ah, thanks for entertaining them," he called out.

Nell lifted her head. He could see her clearly in the stage lights. Clearly enough that he caught the lift of her brow, the coolness of her unsmiling mouth, before she lowered her head again.

Fine, he told himself as he caught both boys on the fly. He didn't want to talk to her anyway.

Chapter 5

She didn't have to ignore him so completely. Mac sipped the cup of hard cider his brother-in-law had pressed on him and resentfully studied Nell's back.

She'd had it turned in his direction for an hour.

A hell of a back, too, he thought, half listening as the mayor rattled on in his ear. Smooth and straight, topped off by the fluid curve of her shoulders. It looked very seductive in the thin plum-colored jacket she wore over a short matching dress.

She had terrific legs. He didn't think he'd

ever actually seen them before. He would have remembered. Every other time he'd run into her she'd had them covered up.

She'd probably worn a dress tonight to torment him.

Mac cut the mayor off in midstream and strode over to her. "Look, this is stupid."

Nell glanced up. She'd been having a pleasant conversation with a group of Mira's friends—and thoroughly enjoying the simple act of ignoring Mira's brother.

"Excuse me?"

"It's just stupid," he repeated.

"The need to raise more money for the arts in public school is stupid?" she asked, well aware he wasn't referring to the topic she'd been discussing.

"What? No. Damn it, you know what I mean."

"I'm sorry." She started to turn back to the circle of very interested faces, but he took her arm and pulled her aside. "Do you want me to cause a scene in your sister's house?" Nell said between her teeth.

"No." He weaved his way through the minglers, around the dining room table and through the kitchen door. His sister was busy replenishing a tray of canapés. "Give us a minute," he ordered Mira.

"Mac, I'm busy here." Distracted, Mira smoothed a hand over her short brunette hair. "Would you find Dave and tell him we're running low on cider?" She sent Nell a frazzled smile. "I thought I was organized."

"Give us a minute," Mac repeated.

Mira let out an impatient breath, but then her eyebrows shot up, drew in. "Well, well," she murmured, amused and clearly delighted. "I'll just get out of your way. I want a closer look at that boy Kim's so excited about." She picked up the tray of finger food and swung through the kitchen door.

Silence fell like a hammer.

"So." Casually, Nell plucked a carrot stick from a bowl. "Something on your mind, Macauley?"

"I don't see why you have to be so…"

"So?" She crunched into the carrot. "What?"

"You're making a point of not talking to me."

She smiled. "Yes, I am."

"It's stupid."

She located an open bottle of white wine, poured some into a glass. After a sip, she smiled again. "I don't think so. It seems to me that, for no discernible reason, I annoy you. Since I'm quite fond of your family, it seems logical and courteous to stay as far out of your way as I possibly can." She sipped again. "Now, is that all? I've been enjoying myself so far this evening."

"You don't annoy me. Exactly." He couldn't find anything to do with his hands, so he settled on taking a carrot stick and breaking it in half. "I'm sorry...for before."

"You're sorry for kissing me, or for behaving like a jerk afterward?"

He tossed the pieces of carrot down. "You're a hard one, Nell."

"Wait." Eyes wide, she pressed a hand to her ear. "I think something's wrong with my hearing. I thought, for just a minute, you actually said my name."

"Cut it out," he said. Then, deliberately: "Nell."

"This is a moment," she declared, and toasted him. "Macauley Taylor has actually initiated a conversation with me, *and* used my name. I'm all aflutter."

"Look." Temper had him rounding the counter. He'd nearly grabbed her before he pushed his anger back. "I just want to clear the air."

Fascinated, she studied his now-impassive face. "That's quite a control button you've got there, Mac. It's admirable. Still, I wonder what would happen if you didn't push it so often."

"A man raising two kids on his own needs control."

"I suppose," she murmured. "Now, if that's all—"

"I'm sorry," he said again.

This time she softened. She was simply no good at holding a grudge. "Okay. Let's just forget it. Friends," she offered, and held out a hand.

He took it. It was so soft, so small, he couldn't make himself give it up again. Her eyes were soft, too, just now. Big, liquid eyes you'd have expected to see on a fawn. "You...look nice."

"Thanks. You too."

"You like the party?"

"I like the people." Her pulse was starting to jump. Damn him. "Your sister's wonderful. So full of energy and ideas."

"You have to watch her." His lips curved slowly. "She'll rope you into one of her projects."

"Too late. She's got me on the arts committee already. And I've been volunteered to help with the recycling campaign."

"The trick is to duck."

"I don't mind, really. I think I'm going to enjoy it." His thumb was brushing over her wrist now, lightly. "Mac, don't start something you don't intend to finish."

Brow creased, he looked down at their joined hands. "I think about you. I don't have time to think about you. I don't want to have time."

It was happening again. The flutters and quivers she seemed to have no control over. "What do you want?"

His gaze lifted, locked with hers. "I'm having some trouble with that."

The kitchen door burst open, and a horde of teenagers piled in, only to be brought up short as Kim, in the lead, stopped on a dime.

Her eyes widened as she watched her uncle drop her teacher's hand, and the two of them jumped apart like a couple of teenagers caught necking on the living room sofa.

"Sorry. Ah, sorry," she repeated, goggling. "We were just..." She turned on her heel and shoved back at her friends. They scooted out, chuckling.

"That ought to add some juice to the grapevine," Nell said wryly. She'd been in town long enough to know that everyone would be speculating about Mac Taylor and Nell Davis by morning. Steadier now, she turned back to him. "Listen, why don't we try this in nice easy stages? You want to go out to dinner tomorrow? See a movie or something?"

Now it was his turn to stare. "A date? Are you asking me out on a date?"

Impatience flickered back. "Yes, a date. It doesn't mean I'm asking to bear you more children. On second thought, let's just quit while we're ahead."

"I want to get my hands on you." Mac heard himself say the words, knew it was too late to take them back.

Nell reached for her wine in self-defense. "Well, that's simple."

"No, it's not."

She braced herself and looked up at him again. "No," she agreed quietly. Just how many times, she wondered, had his face popped into her mind in the past few weeks? She couldn't count them. "It's not simple."

But something had to be done, he decided. A move forward, a move back. Take a step, he ordered himself. See what happens. "I haven't been to a movie without the kids... I can't remember. I could probably line up a sitter."

"All right." She was watching him now almost as carefully as he watched her. "Give me a call if it works out. I'll be home most of tomorrow, correcting papers."

It wasn't the easiest thing, stepping back into the dating pool—however small the pool and however warm the water. It irritated him that he was nervous, almost as much as his niece's grins and questions had irritated when she agreed to baby-sit.

Now, as he climbed the sturdy outside steps to Nell's third-floor apartment, Mac wondered if it would be better all around if they forgot the whole thing.

As he stepped onto her deck, he noted that she'd flanked the door with pots of mums. It was a nice touch, he thought. He always appreciated it when someone who rented one of his homes cared enough to bother with those nice touches.

It was just a movie, he reminded himself, and rapped on the door. When she opened it, he was relieved that she'd dressed casually—a hip-grazing sweater over a pair of those snug leggings Kim liked so much.

Then she smiled and had his mouth going dry.

"Hi. You're right on time. Do you want to come in and see what I've done to your place?"

"It's your place—as long as you pay the rent," he told her, but she was reaching out, taking his hand, drawing him in.

Mac had dispensed with the walls that had made stingy little rooms and had created one flowing space of living, dining and kitchen area. And she'd known what to do with it.

There was a huge L-shaped couch in a bold floral print that should have been shocking, but was, instead, perfect. A small table under the window held a pot of dried autumn leaves. Shelves along one wall held books, a stereo and a small TV, and the sort of knickknacks he knew women liked.

She'd turned the dining area into a combination music room and office, with her desk and a small spinet. A flute lay on a music stand.

"I didn't bring a lot with me from New York," she said as she shrugged into her jacket. "Only what I really cared about. I'm filling in with things from antique shops and flea markets.

"We got a million of them," he murmured. "It looks good." And it did—the old, faded rug on the floor, the fussy priscillas at the windows. "Comfortable."

"Comfortable's very important to me. Ready?"

"Sure."

And it wasn't so hard after all.

He'd asked her to pick the movie, and she'd gone for comedy. It was surprisingly relaxing to sit in the darkened theater and share popcorn and laughter.

He only thought about her as a woman, a very attractive woman, a couple of dozen times.

Going for pizza afterward seemed such a natural progression, he suggested it himself. They competed for a table in the crowded pizzeria with teenagers out on date night.

"So..." Nell stretched out in the booth. "How's Zeke's career in spelling coming along?"

"It's a struggle. He really works at it. It's funny, Zack can spell almost anything you toss at him first time around, but Zeke has to study the word like a scholar with the Dead Sea Scrolls."

"He's good at his arithmetic."

"Yeah." Mac wasn't sure how he felt about her knowing so much about his kids. "They're both taken with you."

"It's mutual." She skimmed a hand through her hair. "It's going to sound odd, but…" She hesitated, not quite sure how to word it. "But that first day at rehearsal, when I looked around and saw them? I had this feeling, this— I don't know, it was like, 'Oh, there you are. I was wondering when you'd show up.' It sounds strange, but it was as if I was expecting them. Now, when Kim comes without them, I feel let down."

"I guess they kind of grow on you."

It was more than that, but she didn't know how to explain. And she wasn't entirely sure Mac would accept the fact that she'd very simply fallen for them. "I get a kick out of them telling me about their school day, showing me their papers."

"First report cards are almost here." His grin flashed. "I'm more nervous than they are."

"People put too much emphasis on grades."

His brows shot up at the comment. "This from a teacher?"

"Individual ability, application, effort, retention. Those things are a lot more important than *A, B* or *C.* But I can tell you, in confidence, that Kim's aceing advanced chorus and music history."

"No kidding?" He felt a quick surge of pride. "She never did that well before. *Bs* mostly."

"Mr. Striker and I have markedly different approaches."

"You're telling me. Word around town is that the chorus is dynamite this year. How'd you pull it off?"

"The kids pull it off," she told him, sitting up when their pizza was served. "My job is to make them think and sing like a team. Not to slam Mr. Striker," she added, taking a generous bite. "But I get the impression he was just putting in time, counting the days until he could retire. If you're going to teach kids, you have to like them, and respect them. There's a lot of talent there, some of it extremely rough." When she laughed, the roses in her cheek bloomed deeper. "And some of those kids will do nothing more than sing in the shower for the rest of their lives—for which the world can be grateful."

"Got some clinkers, huh?"

"Well…" She laughed again. "Yes, I have a few. But they're enjoying themselves. That's what counts. And there are a few, like Kim, who are really something special. I'm sending her and two others for auditions to all-state next week. And after the holiday concert I'm going to hold auditions for the spring musical."

"We haven't had a musical at the high school in three years."

"We're going to have one this year, Buster. And it's going to be terrific."

"It's a lot of work for you."

"I like it. And it's what I'm paid for."

Mac toyed with a second slice. "You really do like it, don't you? The school, the town, the whole bit?"

"Why shouldn't I? It's a fine school, a fine town."

"It ain't Manhattan."

"Exactly."

"Why'd you leave?" He winced. "Sorry, none of my business."

"It's all right. I had a bad year. I guess I was getting restless before that, but the last year was just the pits. They eliminated my job at the school. Economic cutbacks. Downsizing. The arts are always the first to suffer." She shrugged. "Anyway, my roommate got married. I couldn't afford the rent on my own—not if I wanted to eat with any regularity—so I advertised for another one. Took references, gauged personalities." With a sigh, she propped her chin on her elbow. "I thought I was careful. But about three weeks after she moved in, I came home and found that she'd cleaned me out."

Mac stopped eating. "She robbed you?"

"She skinned me. TV, stereo, whatever good jewelry I had, cash, the collection of Limoges boxes I'd started in college. I was really steamed, and then I was shaken. I just wasn't comfortable living there after it happened. Then the guy I'd been seeing for about a year started giving me lectures on my stupidity, my naiveté. As far as he was concerned, I'd gotten exactly what I'd deserved."

"Nice guy," Mac muttered. "Very supportive."

"You bet. In any case, I took a good look at him and our relationship and figured he was right on one level. As long as I was in that rut, with him, I was getting what I deserved. So I decided to climb out of the rut, and leave him in it."

"Good choice."

"I thought so." And so was he, she thought, studying Mac's face. A very good choice. "Why don't you tell me what your plans are with the house you're renovating."

"I don't guess you'd know a lot about plumbing."

She only smiled. "I'm a quick learner."

It was nearly midnight when he pulled up in front of her apartment. He hadn't intended to stay out so late. He certainly hadn't expected to spend more than an hour talking to her about wiring and plumbing and load-bearing walls. Or drawing little blueprints on napkins.

But somehow he'd manage to get through the evening without feeling foolish, or pinned down or out of step. Only one thing worried him. He wanted to see her again.

"I think this was a good first step." She laid a hand over his, kissed his cheek. "Thanks."

"I'll walk you up."

Her hand was already on the door handle. Safer, she'd decided for both of them, if she just hurried along. "You don't have to. I know the way."

"I'll walk you up," he repeated. He stepped out, rounded the hood. They started up the stairs together. The tenant on the first floor was still awake. The mutter of a television, and its ghost gray light, filtered through the window.

Since the breeze had died, it was the only sound. And overhead countless stars wheeled in a clear black sky.

"If we do this again," Mac began, "people in town are going to start talking about us, making out that we're..." He wasn't quite sure of the right phrase.

"An item?" Nell supplied. "That bothers you."

"I don't want the kids to get any ideas, or worry, or...whatever." As they reached the landing, he looked down at her and was caught again. "It must be the way you look," he murmured.

"What must?"

"That makes me think about you." It was a reasonable explanation, he decided. Physical attraction. After all, he wasn't a dead man. He was just a careful one. "That makes me think about doing this."

He cupped her face in his hands—a gesture so sweet, so tender, it had every muscle in her body going lax. It was just as slow, as stunning, as sumptuous, as the first time. The touch of his mouth on hers, the shuddering patience, the simple wonder of it.

Could it be this? she wondered. Could it be this that she'd been waiting for? Could it be him?

He heard her soft, breathy sigh as he eased his mouth from hers. Lingering, he knew, would be a mistake, and he let his hands fall away before they could reach for more.

As if to capture one final taste, Nell ran her

tongue over her lips. "You're awfully good at that, Macauley. Awfully good."

"You could say I've been saving up." But he didn't think it was that at all. He was very much worried it wasn't that. "I'll see you."

She nodded weakly as he headed down the steps. She was still leaning dreamily against the door when she heard his car start and drive away.

For a moment, she would have sworn the air rang with the distant music of sleigh bells.

Chapter 6

The end of October meant parent-teacher conferences, and a much-anticipated holiday for students. It also meant a headache for Mac. He had to juggle the twins from his sister to Kim to Mrs. Hollis, fitting in a trip to order materials and an electrical inspection.

When he turned his truck into the educational complex, he was jumpy with nerves. Lord knew what he was about to be told about his children, how they behaved when they were out of his sight and his control. He worried that he hadn't made enough time to help them with their schoolwork and somehow missed a parental step in preparing them for the social, educational and emotional demands of first grade.

Because of his failure, his boys would become antisocial, illiterate neurotics.

He knew he was being ridiculous, but he couldn't stop his fears from playing over and over like an endless loop in his brain.

"Mac!" The car horn and the sound of his name had him turning and focusing, finally, on his sister's car. She leaned out the window, shaking her head at him. "Where were you? I called you three times."

"Bailing my kids out of jail," he muttered, and changed course to walk to her car. "I've got a conference in a minute."

"I know. I've just come from a meeting at the high school. Remember, we compared schedules."

"Right. I shouldn't be late."

"You don't get demerits. My meeting was about raising funds for new chorus uniforms. Those kids have been wearing the same old choir robes for twelve years. We're hoping to raise enough to put them in something a little snazzier."

"Fine, I'll give you a donation, but I shouldn't be late." Already he was imagining the young, fresh-faced first grade teacher marking him tardy, just another item on a growing list of negatives about Taylor males.

"I just wanted to say that Nell seemed upset about something."

"What?"

"Upset," Mira repeated, pleased that she finally had his full attention. "She came up with a couple of nice ideas for fund-raisers, but she was obviously distracted." Mira lifted a brow, eyeing her brother slyly. "You haven't done anything to annoy her, have you?"

"No." Mac caught himself before he shifted guiltily from foot to foot. "Why should I?"

"Couldn't say. But since you've been seeing her—"

"We went to the movies."

"And for pizza," Mira added. "A couple of Kim's friends spotted you."

The curse of small towns, Mac thought, and stuffed his hands in his pockets. "So?"

"So nothing. Good for you. I like her a lot. Kim's crazy about her. I suppose I'm feeling a bit protective. She was definitely upset, Mac, and trying not to show it. Maybe she'd talk to you about it."

"I'm not going to go poking around in her personal life."

"The way I see it, you're part of her personal life. See you later." She pulled off without giving him a chance for a parting shot.

Muttering to himself, Mac marched up to the elementary school. When he marched out twenty minutes later, he was in a much lighter mood. His children had not been declared social misfits with homicidal tendencies after all. In fact, their teacher had praised them.

Of course, he'd known all along.

Maybe Zeke forgot the rules now and then and talked to his neighbor. And maybe Zack was a little shy about raising his hand when he knew an answer. But they were settling in.

With the weight of first grade off his shoulders, Mac headed out. Impulse had him swinging toward the high school. He knew his conference had been one of the last of the day. He wasn't sure how teachers' meetings worked at the high school, but the lot was nearly empty. He spotted Nell's car, however, and decided it wouldn't hurt just to drop in.

It wasn't until he was inside that he realized he didn't have a clue as to where to find her.

Mac poked his head into the auditorium, but it was empty. Since he'd come that far, he backtracked to the main office and caught one of the secretaries as she was leaving for the day. Following her directions, he turned down a corridor, headed up a ramp and turned right.

Nell's classroom door was open. Not like any classroom he'd done time in, he thought. This one had a piano, music stands, instruments, a tape recorder. There was the usual blackboard, wiped clean, and a desk where Nell was currently working.

He watched her for a long moment, the way her hair fell, the way her fingers held the pen, the way her sweater draped at the neck. It occurred to him that if he'd ever had a teacher who looked like that, he would have been a great deal more interested in music.

"Hi."

Her head snapped up. There was a martial

light in her eyes that surprised him, a stubborn set to her jaw. Even as he watched, she took a long breath and worked up a smile.

"Hello, Mac. Welcome to bedlam."

"Looks like a lot of work." He stepped inside, up to the desk. It was covered with papers, books, computer printouts and sheet music, all in what appeared to be ordered piles.

"Finishing up the first marking period, grades, class planning, fund-raising strategy, fine-tuning the holiday concert—and trying to make the budget stretch to producing the spring musical." Trying to keep her foul mood to herself, she sat back. "So, how was your day?"

"Pretty good. I just had a conference with the twins' teacher. They're doing fine. I can stop sweating report cards."

"They're great kids. You've got nothing to worry about."

"Worry comes with the territory. What are you worried about?" he asked before he could remind himself he wasn't going to pry.

"How much time have you got?" she shot back.

"Enough." Curious, he eased a hip onto the edge of her desk. He wanted to soothe, he discovered, to stroke away that faint line between her brows. "Rough day?"

She jerked her shoulders, then pushed away from her desk. Temper always forced her to move. "I've had better. Do you know how much school and community support the football team gets? All the sports teams." She began to slap cassette tapes into a box—anything to keep her hands busy. "Even the band. But the chorus, we have to go begging for every dollar."

"You're ticked off about the budget?"

"Why shouldn't I be?" She whirled back, eyes hot. "No problem getting equipment for the football team so a bunch of boys can go out on the field and tackle each other, but I have to spend an hour on my knees if I want eighty bucks to get a piano tuned." She caught herself, sighed. "I don't have anything against football. I like it. High school sports are important."

"I know a guy who tunes pianos," Mac said. "He'd probably donate his time."

Nell rubbed a hand over her face, slid it around to soothe the tension at the back of her neck. Dad can fix anything, she thought, just as the twins had claimed. Have a problem? Call Mac.

"That would be great," she said, and managed a real smile. "If I can beat my way through the paperwork and get approval. You can't even take freebies without going through the board." It irritated her, as always. "One of the worst aspects of teaching is the bureaucracy. Maybe I should have stuck with performing in clubs."

"You performed in clubs?"

"In another life," she muttered, waving it away. "A little singing to pay my way through college. It was better than waiting tables. Anyway, it's not the budget, not really. Or even the lack of interest from the community. I'm used to that."

"Do you want to tell me what it is, or do you want to stew about it?"

"I was having a pretty good time stewing about it." She sighed again, and looked up at him. He seemed so solid, so dependable.

"Maybe I'm too much of an urbanite after all. I've had my first run-in with old-fashioned rural attitude, and I'm stumped. Do you know Hank Rohrer?"

"Sure. He has a dairy farm out on Old Oak Road. I think his oldest kid is in the same class as Kim."

"Hank, Jr. Yes. Junior's one of my students—a very strong baritone. He has a real interest in music. He even writes it."

"No kidding? That's great."

"You'd think so, wouldn't you?" Nell tossed her hair back and went to her desk again to tidy her already tidy papers. "Well, I asked Mr. and Mrs. Rohrer to come in this morning because Junior backed out of going to all-state auditions this weekend. I knew he had a very good chance of making it, and I wanted to discuss the possibility with his parents of a music scholarship. When I told them how talented Junior was and how I hoped they'd encourage him to change his mind about the auditions, Hank Senior acted as though I'd just insulted him. He was appalled." There was bitterness in her voice now, as well as anger. "'No son of his was going to waste his time on singing and writing music like some...'"

She trailed off, too furious to repeat the man's opinion of musicians. "They didn't even know Junior was in my class. Thought he was taking shop as his elective this year. I tried to smooth it over, said that Junior needed a fine-art credit to graduate. I didn't do much good. Mr. Rohrer could barely swallow the idea of Junior staying in my class. He went on about how Junior didn't need singing lessons to run a farm. And he certainly wasn't going to allow him to take a Saturday and go audition when the boy had chores. And I'm to stop putting any fancy ideas about college in the boy's head."

"They've got four kids," Mac said slowly. "Tuition might be a problem."

"If that were the only obstacle, they should be grateful for the possibility of scholarship." She slapped her grade book closed. "What we have is a bright, talented boy who has dreams, dreams he'll never be able to explore because his parents won't permit it. Or his father won't," she added. "His mother didn't say two words the entire time they were here."

"Could be she'll work on Hank once she has him alone."

"Could be he'll take out his annoyance with me on both of them."

"Hank's not like that. He's set in his ways and thinks he knows all the answers, but he isn't mean."

"It's a little tough for me to see his virtues after he called me—" she had to take a deep breath "—a slick-handed flatlander who's wasting his hard-earned tax dollars. I could have made a difference with that boy," Nell murmured as she sat again. "I know it."

"So maybe you won't be able to make a difference with Junior. You'll make a difference with someone else. You've already made one with Kim."

"Thanks." Nell's smile was brief. "That helps a little."

"I mean it." He hated to see her this way, all that brilliant energy and optimism dimmed. "She's gained a lot of confidence in herself. She's always been shy about her singing, about a lot of things. Now she's really opening up."

It did help to hear it. This time Nell's smile came easier. "So I should stop brooding."

"It doesn't suit you." He surprised himself, and her, by reaching down to run his knuckles over her cheek. "Smiling does."

"I've never been able to hold on to temperament for long. Bob used to say it was because I was shallow."

"Who the hell's Bob?"

"The one who's still in the rut."

"Clearly where he belongs."

She laughed. "I'm glad you dropped by. I'd have probably sat here for another hour clenching my jaw."

"It's a pretty jaw," Mac murmured, then shifted away. "I've got to get going. I've got Halloween costumes to put together."

"Need any help?"

"I..." It was tempting, too tempting, and far too dangerous, he thought, to start sharing family traditions with her. "No, I've got it covered."

Nell accepted the disappointment, nearly

masked it. "You'll bring them by Saturday night, won't you? To trick-or-treat?"

"Sure. I'll see you." He started out but stopped at the doorway and turned back. "Nell?"

"Yes?"

"Some things take a while to change. Change makes some people nervous."

She tilted her head. "Are you talking about the Rohrers, Mac?"

"Among others. I'll see you Saturday night."

Nell studied the empty doorway as his footsteps echoed away. Did he think she was trying to change him? Was she? She sat back, pushing away from the paperwork. She'd never be able to concentrate on it now.

Whenever she was around Macauley Taylor, it was hard to concentrate. When had she become so susceptible to the slow, thorough, quiet type? From the moment he'd walked into the auditorium to pick up Kim and the twins, she admitted.

Love at first sight? Surely she was too sophisticated, too smart, to believe in such a thing. And surely, she added, she was too smart to put herself in the vulnerable position of falling in love with a man who didn't return her feelings.

Or didn't want to, she thought. And that was even worse.

It couldn't matter that he was sweet and kind and devoted to his children. It shouldn't matter that he was handsome and strong and sexy. She wouldn't let it matter that being with him, thinking of him, had her longing for things. For home, for family, for laughter in the kitchen and passion in bed.

She let out a long breath, because it did matter. It mattered very much when a woman was teetering right on the edge of falling in love.

Chapter 7

Mid-November had stripped the leaves from the trees. There was a beauty even in this, Nell had decided. Beauty in the dark, denuded branches, in the papery rustle of dried leaves along the curbs, in the frost that shimmered like diamond dust on the grass in the mornings.

She caught herself staring out of the window too often, wishing for snow like a child hoping for a school holiday.

It felt wonderful. Wonderful to anticipate the winter, to remember the fall. She often thought about Halloween night, and all the children who had come knocking on her door dressed as pirates and princesses. She remembered the way Zeke and Zack had giggled when she pretended not to recognize them in the elaborate astronaut costumes Mac had fashioned for them.

She found herself reminiscing about the bluegrass concert Mac had taken her to. Or the fun they'd had when she ran into him and the boys at the mall just last week, all of them on a mission to complete their Christmas lists early.

Now, strolling past the house Mac was remodeling, she thought of him again. It had been so sweet, the way he'd struggled over chosing just the right outfit for Kim's present. No thoughtless gifts from Macauley Taylor for those he cared about. It had to be the right color, the right style.

She'd come to believe everything about him was right.

She passed the house, drawing in the chilly air of evening, her mood buoyant. That afternoon she'd been proud to announce that two of her students would participate in all-state chorus.

She had made a difference, Nell thought, shutting her eyes on the pleasure of it. Not just the prestige, certainly not simply the delight of having the principal congratulate her. The difference, the important one, had been the look on her students' faces. The pride, not just on Kim's face and that of the tenor who would go to all-state with her. But on the faces of the entire chorus. They all shared in the triumph, because over the past few weeks they had become a team.

Her team. Her kids.

"It's cold for walking."

Nell jolted, tensed, then laughed at herself when she saw Mac step away from the shadow of a tree in his sister's yard. "Lord, you gave me a start. I nearly went into my repel-the-mugger stance."

"Taylor's Grove's a little sparse when it comes to muggers. Are you going to see Mira?"

"No, actually, I was just out walking. Too much energy to stay in." The smile lit her face. "You've heard the good news?"

"Congratulations."

"It's not me—"

"Yeah, it is. A lot of it." It was the only way he knew to tell her how proud he was of what she'd done. He glanced back toward the house, where lights gleamed. "Mira and Kim are in there crying."

"Crying? But—"

"Not that kind of crying." Female tears always embarrassed him. He shrugged. "You know, the other kind."

"Oh." In response, Nell felt her own eyes sting. "That's nice."

"Dave's going around with a big fat grin on his face. He was talking to his parents when I ducked out. Mira's already called ours, as well as every other friend and relative in the country."

"Well, it's a big deal."

"I know it is." His teeth flashed. "I've made a few calls myself. You must be feeling pretty pleased with yourself."

"You bet I am. Seeing the kids today when I made the announcement…well, it was the best. And it's a hell of a kickoff for our fundraiser." She shivered as the wind shuddered through the trees.

"You're getting cold. I'll drive you home."

"That'd be nice. I keep waiting for snow."

In the way of every countryman since Adam, he sniffed the air, checked out the sky. "You won't have to wait much longer." He opened the truck door for her. "The kids have already gotten their sleds out."

"I might buy one for myself." She settled back, relaxed. "Where are the boys?"

"There's a sleepover at one of their friends'." He gestured toward the house across the street from Mira's. "I just dropped them off."

"They must be thinking a lot about Christmas now, with snow in the air."

"It's funny. Usually right after Halloween they start barraging me with lists and pictures of toys from catalogs, stuff they see on TV." He turned the truck and headed for the square. "This year they told me Santa's taking care of it. I know they want bikes." His brow creased. "That's all I've heard. They've been whispering together about something else, but they clam up when I come around."

"That's Christmas," Nell said easily. "It's

the best time for whispers and secrets. What about you?" She turned to smile at him. "What do you want for Christmas?"

"More than the two hours' sleep I usually get."

"You can do better than that."

"When the kids come downstairs in the morning, and their faces light up, I've got all I want." He stopped in front of her apartment. "Are you going back to New York for the holiday?"

"No, there's nothing there."

"Your family?"

"I'm an only child. My parents usually spend the holiday in the Caribbean. Do you want to come in, have some coffee?"

It was a much more appealing idea than going home to an empty house. "Yeah, thanks." When they started up the stairs, he tried to swing tactfully back to the holidays and her family. "Is that where you spent Christmas as a kid? In the Caribbean?"

"No. We had a fairly traditional setting in Philadelphia. Then I went to school in New York, and they moved to Florida." She opened the door and took off her coat. "We aren't very close, really. They weren't terribly happy with my decision to study music."

"Oh." He tossed his jacket over hers while she moved into the kitchen to put on the coffee. "I guess that's why you got so steamed about Junior."

"Maybe. They didn't really disapprove so much as they were baffled. We get along much better long-distance." She glanced over her shoulder. "I think that's why I admire you."

He stopped studying the rosewood music box on a table and stared at her. "Me?"

"Your interest and involvement with your children, your whole family. It's so solid, so natural." Tossing back her hair, she reached into the cookie jar and began to spread cookies on a plate. "Not everyone is as willing, or as able, to put in so much time and attention. Not everyone loves as well, or as thoroughly." She smiled. "Now I've embarrassed you."

"No. Yes," he admitted, and took one of the cookies. "You haven't asked about their mother." When she said nothing, Mac found himself talking. "I was just out of college when I met her. She was a secretary in my father's real estate office. She was beautiful. I mean eye-popping beautiful, the kind that bowls you over. We went out a couple of times, we went to bed, she got pregnant."

The flat-voiced recitation had Nell looking up. Mac bit into the cookie, tasting bitterness. "I know that sounds like she did it on her own. I was young, but I was old enough to know what I was doing, old enough to be responsible."

He had always taken his responsibilities seriously, Nell thought, and he always would. You only had to look at him to see the dependability.

"You didn't say anything about love."

"No, I didn't." It was something he didn't take lightly. "I was attracted, so was she. Or I thought she was. What I didn't know was that she'd lied about using birth control. It wasn't until after I'd married her that I found out she'd set out to 'snag the boss's son.' Her words," he added. "Angie saw an opportunity to improve her standard of living."

It surprised him that even now, after all this

time, it hurt both pride and heart to know he'd been so carelessly used.

"To make a long story short," he continued, in that same expressionless tone, "she hadn't counted on twins, or the hassle of motherhood. So, about a month after the boys were born, she cleaned out my bank account and split."

"I'm so sorry, Mac," Nell murmured. She wished she knew the words, the gesture, that would erase that cool dispassion from his eyes. "It must have been horrible for you."

"It could have been worse." His eyes met Nell's briefly before he shrugged it off. "I could have loved her. She contacted me once, telling me she wanted me to foot the bill for the divorce. In exchange for that, I could have the kids free and clear. Free and clear," he repeated. "As if they were stocks and bonds instead of children. I took her up on it. End of story."

"Is it?" Nell moved to him, took his hands in hers. "Even if you didn't love her, she hurt you."

She rose on her toes to kiss his cheek, to

soothe, to comfort. She saw the change in his eyes—and, yes, the hurt in them. It explained a great deal, she thought, to hear him tell the story. To see his face as he did. He'd been disillusioned, devastated. Instead of giving in to it, or leaning on his parents for help with the burden, he'd taken his sons and started a life with them. A life for them.

"She didn't deserve you, or the boys."

"It wasn't a hardship." He couldn't take his eyes off hers now. It wasn't the sympathy so much as the simple, unquestioning understanding that pulled at him. "They're the best part of me. I didn't mean it to sound like it was a sacrifice."

"You didn't. You don't." Her heart melted as she slid her arms around him. She'd meant that, too, as a comfort. But something more, something deeper, was stirring inside her. "You made it sound as if you love them. It's very appealing to hear a man say that he thinks of his children as a gift. And to know he means it."

He was holding her, and he wasn't quite sure how it had happened. It seemed so easy, so natural, to have her settled in his arms. "When you're given a gift, an important one, you have to be careful with it." His voice thickened with a mix of emotions. His children. Her. Something about the way she was looking up at him, the way her lips curved. He lifted a hand to stroke her hair, lingered over it a moment before he remembered to back away. "I should go."

"Stay." It was so easy, she discovered, to ask him. So easy, after all, to need him. "You know I want you to stay. You know I want you."

He couldn't take his eyes off her face, and the need was so much bigger, so much sweeter, than he'd ever imagined. "It could complicate things, Nell. I've got a lot of baggage. Most of it's in storage, but—"

"I don't care." Her breath trembled out. "I don't even have any pride at the moment. Make love with me, Mac." On a sigh, she pulled his head down and pressed her lips to his. "Just love me tonight."

He couldn't resist. It was a fantasy that had begun to wind through him, body and mind, the moment he first met her. She was all softness, all warmth. He'd done without both of those miraculous female gifts for so long.

Now, with her mouth on his and her arms twined around him, she was all he could want.

He'd never considered himself romantic. He wondered if a woman like Nell would prefer candlelight, soft music, perfumed air. But the scene was already set. He could do nothing more than lift her into his arms and carry her to the bedroom.

He turned on a lamp, surprised at how suddenly his nerves vanished when he saw hers reflected in her eyes.

"I've thought about this a long time," he told her. "I want to see you, every minute I'm touching you. I want to see you."

"Good." She looked up at him and his smile soothed away some of her tension. "I want to see you."

He carried her to the bed and lay down beside her, stroking a hand through her hair, over her shoulders. Then he dipped his head to kiss her.

It was so easy, as if they had shared nights

and intimacy for years. It was so thrilling, as if each of them had come to the bed as innocent as a babe.

A touch, a taste, patient and lingering. A murmur, a sigh, soft and quiet. His hands never rushed, only pleasured, stroking over her, unfastening buttons, pausing to explore.

Her skin quivered under his caress even as it heated. A hundred pulse points thrummed, speeding at the brush of a fingertip, the flick of a tongue. Her own hands trembled, pulling a laughing groan from her that ended on a broken whimper when she at last found flesh.

Making love. The phrase had never been truer to her. For here was an exquisite tenderness mixed with a lustful curiosity that overpowered the senses, tangled in the system like silken knots. Each time his mouth returned to hers, it went deeper, wider, higher, so that he was all that existed for her. All that needed to.

She gave with a depthless generosity that staggered him. She fit, body to body, with him, with a perfection that thrilled. Each time he thought his control would slip, he found himself sliding easily back into the rhythm they set.

Slow, subtle, savoring.

She was small, delicately built. The fragility he sensed made his hands all the more tender. Even as she arched and cried out the first time, he didn't hurry. It was gloriously arousing for him simply to watch her face, that incredibly expressive face, as every emotion played over it.

He fought back the need to bury himself inside her, clung to control long enough to protect them both. Their eyes locked when at last he slipped into her. Her breath caught and released, and then her lips curved.

Outside, the wind played against the windows, making a music like sleigh bells. And the first snow of the season began to fall as quietly as a wish.

Chapter 8

He couldn't get enough of her. Mac figured at worst it was a kind of insanity, at best a temporary obsession. No matter how many demands there were on his time, his brain, his emotions, he still found odd moments, day and night, to think about Nell.

Though he knew it was cynical, he wished it could have been just sex. If it was only sex, he could put it down to hormones and get back to business. But he didn't just imagine her in bed, or fantasize about finding an hour to lose himself in that trim little body.

Sometimes, when she slipped into his head,

she was standing in front of a group of children, directing their voices with her hands, her arms, her whole self. Or she'd be seated at the piano, with his boys on either side of her, laughing with them. Or she'd just be walking through town, with her hands in her pockets and her face lifted toward the sky.

She scared him right down to the bone.

And she, he thought as he measured his baseboard trim, she was so easy about the whole thing. That was a woman for you, he decided. They didn't have to worry about making the right moves, saying the right thing. They just had to...to be, he thought. That was enough to drive a man crazy.

He couldn't afford to be crazy. He had kids to raise, a business to run. Hell, he had laundry to do if he ever got home. And damn it, he'd forgotten to take the chicken out of the freezer again.

They'd catch burgers on the way to the concert, he told himself. He had enough on his mind without having to fix dinner. Christmas was barreling toward him, and the kids were acting strange.

Just the bikes, Dad, they told him. Santa's making them, and he's taking care of the big present.

What big present? Mac wondered. No interrogation, no tricks, had pulled out that particular answer. For once his kids were closed up tight. That was an idea that disturbed him. He knew that in another year, two if he was lucky, they'd begin to question and doubt the existence of Santa and magic. The end of innocence. Whatever it was they were counting on for Christmas morning, he wanted to see that they found it under the tree.

But they just grinned at him when he prodded and told him it was a surprise for all three of them.

He'd have to work on it. Mac hammered the trim into place. At least they'd gotten the tree up and baked some cookies, strung the popcorn. He felt a little twinge of guilt over the fact that he'd evaded Nell's offer to help with the decorating. And ignored the kids when they asked if she could come over and trim the tree with them.

Was he the only one who could see what a

mistake it would be to have his children become too attached? She'd only been in town for a few months. She could leave at any time. Nell might find them cute, attractive kids, but she didn't have any investment in them.

Damn it, now *he* was making them sound like stocks and bonds.

It wasn't what he meant, Mac assured himself. He simply wasn't going to allow anyone to walk out on his sons again.

He wouldn't risk it, not for anything in heaven or on earth.

After nailing the last piece of baseboard in place, he nodded in approval. The house was coming together just fine. He knew what he was doing there. Just as he knew what he was doing with the boys.

He only wished he had a better idea of what to do with Nell.

"Maybe it'll happen tonight." Zeke watched his breath puff out like smoke as he and his twin sat in the tree house, wrapped against the December chill in coats and scarves.

"It's not Christmas yet."

"But it's the Christmas concert," Zeke said stubbornly. He was tired of waiting for the mom. "That's where we saw her first. And they'll have the music and the tree and stuff, so it'll be like Christmas."

"I don't know." Zack liked the idea, a lot, but was more cautious. "Maybe, but we don't get any presents until Christmas."

"We do, too. When Mr. Perkins pretends to be Santa at the party at the firehouse. That's whole weeks before Christmas, and he gives all the kids presents."

"Not *real* presents. Not stuff you ask for." But Zack set his mind to it. "Maybe if we wish real hard. Dad likes her a lot. Aunt Mira was telling Uncle Dave that Dad's found the right woman even if he doesn't know it." Zack's brow creased. "How could he not know it if he found her?"

"Aunt Mira's always saying stuff that doesn't make sense," Zeke said, with the easy disdain of the young. "Dad's going to marry her, and she's going to come live with us and be the mom. She has to be. We've been good, haven't we?"

"Uh-huh." Zack played with the toe of his boot. "Do you think she'll love us and all that?"

"Probably." Zeke shot his twin a look. "I love her already."

"Me too." Zack smiled in relief. Everything was going to be okay after all.

"All right, people." Nell pitched her voice above the din in the chorus room. It doubled as backstage on concert nights, and students were swarming around, checking clothes, makeup and hair and working off preperformance jitters by talking at the top of their lungs. "Settle down."

One of her students had his head between his knees, fighting off acute stage fright. Nell sent him a sympathetic smile as her group began to quiet.

"You've all worked really hard for tonight. I know a lot of you are jumpy because you have friends and family out in the audience. Use the nerves to sharpen your performance. Please try to remember to go out onstage in the organized, dignified manner we've practiced."

There were some snickers at that. Nell merely lifted a brow. "I should have said remember to be more dignified and more orderly than you've managed at practice. Diaphragms," she said. "Projection. Posture. Smiles." She paused, lifted a hand. "And above all, I expect you to remember the most vital ingredient in tonight's performance. Enjoy it," she said, and grinned. "It's Christmas. Now let's go knock 'em dead."

Her heart was doing some pretty fancy pumping of its own as she directed the children onstage, watched them take their positions on the risers as the murmurs from the audience rose and ebbed. For many, Nell knew, this concert would be her first test. Decisions from the community would be made tonight as to whether the school board had made a good or a bad choice in their new music teacher.

She took a deep breath, tugged at the hem of her velvet jacket and stepped onstage.

There was polite applause as she approached the solo mike.

"Welcome to Taylor's Grove High School's holiday concert," she began.

"Gosh, Dad, doesn't Miss Davis look pretty?"

"Yeah, Zack, she does." *Lovely* was more the word, he thought, in that soft-looking deep forest green suit, with holly berries in her hair and a quick, nervous smile on her face.

She looked terrific in the spotlight. He wondered if she knew it.

At the moment, all Nell knew was nerves. She wished she could see faces clearly. She'd always preferred seeing her audience when she was performing. It made it more intimate, more fun. After her announcement, she turned, saw every student's eyes on hers, then smiled in reassurance.

"Okay, kids," she murmured, in an undertone only they could hear. "Let's rock."

She started them off with a bang, the Springsteen number, and it had eyes popping wide in the audience. This was not the usual yawn-inspiring program most had been expecting.

When the applause hit, Nell felt the tension dissolve. They'd crossed the first hurdle. She segued from the fun to the traditional, thrilled when the auditorium filled with the harmony on "Cantate Domine," delighted when her sopranos soared on "Adeste Fideles," grinning when they bounced into "Jingle Bell Rock," complete with the little stage business of swaying and hand clapping they'd worked on.

And her heart swelled when Kim approached the mike and the first pure notes of her solo flowed into the air.

"Oh, Dave." Sniffling, Mira clutched her husband's hand, then Mac's. "Our baby."

Nell's prediction had been on target. When Kim stepped back in position, there were damp eyes in every row. They closed the concert with "Silent Night," only voices, no piano. The way it was meant to be sung, Nell had told her students. The way it was written to be sung.

When the last note died and she turned to gesture to her chorus, the audience was already on its feet. The kick of it jolted through her as she turned her head, saw the slack jaws, wide eyes and foolish grins of her students.

Nell swallowed tears, waiting until the noise abated slightly before crossing to the mike again. She knew how to play it.

"They were terrific, weren't they?"

As she'd hoped, that started the cheers and applause all over again. She waited it out.

"I'd like to thank you all for coming, for supporting the chorus. I owe a special thanks to the parents of the singers onstage tonight for their patience, their understanding, and their willingness to let me share their children for a few hours every day. Every student onstage has worked tremendously hard for tonight, and I'm delighted that you appreciate their talent, and their effort. I'd like to add that the poinsettias you see onstage were donated by Hill Florists and are for sale at three dollars a pot. Proceeds to go to the fund for new choir uniforms. Merry Christmas, and come back."

Before she could step away from the mike, Kim and Brad were standing on either side of her.

"There's just one more thing." Brad cleared his throat until the rustling in the audience died down. "The chorus would like to present a token of appreciation to Miss Davis for all her work and encouragement. Ah..." Kim had

written the speech out, but Brad had been des-
ignated to say it. He fumbled a little, grinned
self-consciously at Kim. "This is Miss Davis's
first concert at Taylor High. Ah..." He just
couldn't remember all the nice words Kim had
written, so he said what he felt. "She's the
best. Thanks, Miss Davis."

"We hope you like it," Kim murmured under the applause as she handed Nell a brightly
wrapped box. "All the kids chipped in."

"I'm..." She didn't know what to say, was
afraid to try. When she opened the box, she
stared, misty-eyed, down at a pin shaped like
a treble clef.

"We know you like jewelry," Kim began.
"So we thought—"

"It's beautiful. It's perfect." Taking a
steadying breath, she turned to the chorus.
"Thanks. It means almost as much to me as
you do. Merry Christmas."

"She got a present," Zack pointed out.
They were waiting in the crowded corridor
outside the auditorium to congratulate Kim.
"That means we could get one tonight. We
could get her."

"Not if she goes home right after." Zack had already worked this out. He was waiting for his moment. When he saw her, he pounced. "Miss Davis! Over here, Miss Davis!"

Mac didn't move. Couldn't. Something had happened while he sat three rows back, watching her on the stage. Seeing her smile, seeing tears in her eyes. Just seeing her.

He was in love with her. It was nothing he'd ever experienced. Nothing he knew how to handle. Running seemed the smartest solution, but he didn't think he could move.

"Hi!" She crouched down for hugs, squeezing the boys tight, kissing each cheek. "Did you like the concert?"

"It was real good. Kim was the best."

Nell leaned close to Zeke's ear. "I think so, too, but it has to be a secret."

"We're good at keeping secrets." He smiled smugly at his brother. "We've had one for weeks and weeks."

"Can you come to our house now, Miss Davis?" Zack clung to her hand and put all his charm into his eyes. "Please? Come see our tree and the lights. We put lights everywhere so you can see them from all the way down on the road."

"I'd like that." Testing the water, she glanced up at Mac. "But your dad might be tired."

He wasn't tired, he was flattened. Her lashes were still damp, and the little pin the kids had given her glinted against her velvet jacket. "You're welcome to come out, if you don't mind the drive."

"I'd like it. I'm still wired up." She straightened, searching for some sign of welcome or rebuff in Mac's face. "If you're sure it isn't a bad time."

"No." His tongue was thick, he realized. As if he'd been drinking. "I want to talk to you."

"I'll head out as soon as I'm finished here, then." She winked at the boys and melted back into the crowd.

"She's done wonders with those kids." Mrs. Hollis nodded to Mac. "It'll be a shame to lose her."

"Lose her?" Mac glanced down at his boys, but they were already in a huddle, exchanging whispers. "What do you mean?"

"I heard from Mr. Perkins, who got it from Addie McVie at the high school office, that Nell Davis was offered her old position back at that New York school starting next fall. Nell and the principal had themselves a conference just this morning." Mrs. Hollis babbled on as Mac stared blankly over her head. "Hate to think about her leaving us. Made a difference with these kids." She spied one of her gossip buddies and elbowed her way through the crowd.

Chapter 9

Control came easily to Mac—or at least it had for the past seven years. He used all the control at his disposal to keep his foul mood and bubbling temper from the boys.

They were so excited about her coming, he thought bitterly. Wanted to make certain all the lights were lit, the cookies were out, the decorative bell was hung on Zark's collar.

They were in love with her, too, he realized. And that made it a hell of a mess.

He should have known better. He *had* known better. Somehow he'd let it happen anyway. Let himself slip, let himself fall. And he'd dragged his kids along with him.

Well, he'd have to fix it, wouldn't he? Mac got himself a beer, tipped the bottle back. He was good at fixing things.

"Ladies like wine," Zack informed him. "Like Aunt Mira does."

He remembered Nell had sipped white wine at Mira's party. "I don't have any," he muttered.

Because his father looked unhappy, Zack hugged Mac's leg. "You can buy some before she comes over next time."

Reaching down, Mac cupped his son's upturned face. The love was so strong, so vital, Mac could all but feel it grip him by the throat. "Always got an answer, don't you, pal?"

"You like her, don't you, Dad?"

"Yeah, she's nice."

"And she likes us, too, right?"

"Hey, who wouldn't like the Taylor guys?" He sat at the kitchen table, pulled Zack into his lap. He'd discovered when his sons were infants that there was nothing more magical than holding your own child. "Most of the time *I* even like you."

That made Zack giggle and cuddle closer. "She has to live all by herself, though." Zack began to play with the buttons of his father's shirt. A sure sign, Mac knew, that he was leading up to something.

"Lots of people live alone."

"We've got a big house, and two whole rooms nobody sleeps in except when Grandma and Pop come to visit."

His radar was humming. Mac tugged on his son's ear. "Zack, what are you getting at?"

"Nothing." Lip poked out, Zack toyed with another button. "I was just wondering what it would be like if she came and lived here." He peeked up under his lashes. "So she wouldn't be lonely."

"Nobody said she was lonely," Mac pointed out. "And I think you should—"

The doorbell rang, sending the dog into a fit of excited barking and jingling. Zeke flew into the kitchen, dancing from foot to foot. "She's here! She's here!"

"I got the picture." Mac ruffled Zack's hair, set him on his feet. "Well, let her in. It's cold out."

"I'll do it!"

"*I'll* do it!"

The twins had a fierce race through the house to the front door. They hit it together, fought over the knob, then all but dragged Nell over the threshold once they'd yanked the door open.

"You took so long," Zeke complained. "We've been waiting forever. I put on Christmas music. Hear? And we've got the tree lit and everything."

"So I see." It was a lovely room, one she tried not to resent having only now been invited into.

She knew Mac had built most of the house himself. He'd told her that much. He'd created an open, homey space, with lots of wood, a glass-fronted fireplace where stockings were already hung. The tree, a six-foot blue spruce, was wildly decorated and placed with pride in front of the wide front window.

"It's terrific." Letting the boys pull her along, Nell crossed over to give the tree a closer look. "Really wonderful. It makes the little one in my apartment look scrawny."

"You can share ours." Zack looked up at her, his heart in his eyes. "We can get you a stocking and everything, and have your name put on it."

"They do it at the mall," Zeke told her. "We'll get you a big one."

Now they were pulling at her heart, as well as her hands. Filled with the emotion of the moment, she crouched down to hug them to her. "You guys are the best." She laughed as Zark pushed in for attention. "You, too." Her arms full of kids and dog, she looked up to smile at Mac as he stepped in from the kitchen. "Hi. Sorry I took so long. Some of the kids hung around, wanting to go over every mistake and triumph of the concert."

She shouldn't look so right, so perfect, snuggling his boys under the tree. "I didn't hear any mistakes."

"They were there. But we'll work on them."

She scooted back, sitting on a hassock and taking both boys with her. As if, Mac thought, she meant to keep them.

"We don't have any wine," Zack informed her solemnly. "But we have milk and juice and sodas and beer. Lots of other things. Or..." He cast a crafty look in his father's direction. "Somebody could make hot cocoa."

"One of my specialties." Nell stood to shrug out of her coat. "Where's the kitchen?"

"I'll make it," Mac muttered.

"I'll help." Baffled by his sudden distance, she walked to him. "Or don't you like women in your kitchen?"

"We don't get many around here. You looked good up onstage."

"Thanks. It felt good being there."

He looked past her, into the wide, anticipation-filled eyes of his children. "Why don't you two go change into your pajamas? The cocoa'll be finished by the time you are."

"We'll be faster," Zeke vowed, and shot toward the stairs.

"Only if you throw your clothes on the floor. And don't." He turned back into the kitchen.

"Will they hang them up, or push them under the bed?" Nell asked.

"Zack'll hang them up and they'll fall on the floor. Zeke'll push them under the bed."

She laughed, watching him get out milk and cocoa. "I meant to tell you, a few days ago they came in with Kim to rehearsal. They'd switched sweaters—you know, the color code. I really impressed them when I knew who was who anyway."

He paused in the act of measuring cocoa into a pan. "How did you?"

"I guess I didn't think about it. They're each their own person. Facial expressions. You know how Zeke's eyes narrow and Zack looks under his lashes when they're pleased about something. Inflections in the voice." She opened a cupboard at random, looking for mugs. "Posture. There are all sorts of little clues if you pay attention and look closely enough. Ah, found them." Pleased with herself, she took out four mugs and set them on the counter. She tilted her head when she saw him studying her. Analytically, she thought. As if she were something to be measured and fit into place. "Is something wrong?"

"I wanted to talk to you." He busied himself with heating the cocoa.

"So you said." She found she needed to

steady herself with a hand on the counter. "Mac, am I misreading something, or are you pulling back?"

"I don't know that I'd call it that."

Something was going to hurt. Nell braced for it. "What would you call it?" she said, as calmly as she could.

"I'm a little concerned about the boys. About the fallout when you move on. They're getting too involved." Why did that sound so stupid? he wondered. Why did he feel so stupid?

"*They* are?"

"I think we've been sending the wrong signals, and it would be best for them if we backed off." He concentrated on the cocoa as if it were a nuclear experiment. "We've gone out a few times, and we've…"

"Slept together," she finished, cool now. It was the last defense.

He looked around, sharply. But he could still hear the stomping of little feet in the room overhead. "Yeah. We've slept together, and it was great. The thing is, kids pick up on more things than most people think. And they get ideas. They get attached."

"And you don't want them to get attached to me." Yes, she realized. It was going to hurt. "You don't want to get attached."

"I just think it would be a mistake to take it any further."

"Clear enough. The No Trespassing signs are back up, and I'm out."

"It's not like that, Nell." He set the spoon down, took a step toward her. But there was a line he couldn't quite cross. A line he'd created himself. If he didn't make certain they both stayed on their own sides of it, the life he'd so carefully built could crumble. "I've got things under control here, and I need to keep them that way. I'm all they've got. They're all I've got. I can't mess that up."

"No explanations necessary." Her voice had thickened. In a moment, she knew, it would begin to shake. "You made it clear from the beginning. Crystal-clear. Funny, the first time you invite me into your home, it's to toss me out."

"I'm not tossing you out, I'm trying to re-align things."

"Oh, go to hell, and keep your realignments

for your houses." She sprinted out of the kitchen.

"Nell, don't go like this." But by the time he reached the living room, she was grabbing her coat, and his boys were racing down the stairs.

"Where are you going, Miss Davis? You haven't—" Both boys stopped, shocked by the tears streaming down her face.

"I'm sorry." It was too late to hide them, so she kept heading for the door. "I have to do something. I'm sorry."

And she was gone, with Mac standing impotently in the living room and both boys staring at him. A dozen excuses spun around in his head. Even as he tried to grab one, Zack burst into tears.

"She went away. You made her cry, and she went away."

"I didn't mean to. She—" He moved to gather his sons up and was met with a solid wall of resistance.

"You ruined everything." A tear spilled out of Zeke's eyes, heated by temper. "We did everything we were supposed to, and you ruined it."

"She'll never come back." Zack sat on the bottom step and sobbed. "She'll never be the mom now."

"What?" At his wits' end, Mac dragged his hand through his hair. "What are you two talking about?"

"You ruined it," Zeke said again.

"Look, Miss Davis and I had a... disagreement. People have disagreements. It's not the end of the world." He wished it didn't feel like the end of his world.

"Santa sent her." Zack rubbed his eyes with his fists. "He sent her, just like we asked him. And now she's gone."

"What do you mean, Santa sent her?" Determined, Mac sat on the steps. He pulled a reluctant Zack into his lap and tugged Zeke down to join them. "Miss Davis came from New York to teach music, not from the North Pole."

"We know that." Temper set aside, Zeke sought comfort, turning his face into his father's chest. "She came because we sent Santa a letter, months and months ago, so we'd be early and he'd have time."

"Have time for what?"

"To pick out the mom." On a shuddering sigh, Zack sniffed and looked up at his father. "We wanted someone nice, who smelled good and liked dogs and had yellow hair. And we asked, and she came. And you were supposed to marry her and make her the mom."

Mac let out a long breath and prayed for wisdom. "Why didn't you tell me you were thinking about having a mother?"

"Not *a* mom," Zeke told him. "*The* mom. Miss Davis is the mom, but she's gone now. We love her, and she won't like us anymore because you made her cry."

"Of course she'll still like you." She'd hate him, but she wouldn't take it out on the boys. "But you two are old enough to know you don't get moms from Santa."

"He sent her, just like we asked him. We didn't ask for anything else but the bikes." Zack burrowed into his lap. "We didn't ask for any toys or any games. Just the mom. Make her come back, Dad. Fix it. You always fix it."

"It doesn't work like that, pal. People aren't

broken toys or old houses. Santa didn't send
her, she moved here for a job."

"He did too send her." With surprising dignity, Zack pushed off his father's lap. "Maybe
you don't want her, but we do."

His sons walked up the stairs, a united front
that closed him out. Mac was left with emptiness in the pit of his stomach and the smell
of burned cocoa.

Chapter 10

She should get out of town for a few days, Nell thought. Go somewhere. Go anywhere. There was nothing more pathetic than sitting alone on Christmas Eve and watching other people bustle along the street outside your window.

She'd turned down every holiday party invitation, made excuses that sounded hollow even to her. She was brooding, she admitted, and it was entirely unlike her. But then again, she'd never had a broken heart to nurse before.

With Bob it had been wounded pride. And that had healed itself with embarrassing speed.

Now she was left with bleeding emotions at the time of year when love was most important.

She missed him. Oh, she hated to know that she missed him. That slow, hesitant smile, the quiet voice, the gentleness of him. In New York, at least, she could have lost herself in the crowds, in the rush. But here, everywhere she looked was another reminder.

Go somewhere, Nell. Just get in the car and drive.

She ached to see the children. Wondered if they'd taken their sleds out in the fresh snow that had fallen yesterday. Were they counting the hours until Christmas, plotting to stay awake until they heard reindeer on the roof?

She had presents for them, wrapped and under her tree. She'd send them via Kim or Mira, she thought, and was miserable all over again because she wouldn't see their faces as they tore off the wrappings.

They're not your children, she reminded herself. On that point Mac had always been clear. Sharing himself had been difficult enough. Sharing his children had stopped him dead.

She would go away, she decided, and forced herself to move. She would pack a bag, toss it in the car and drive until she felt like stopping. She'd take a couple of days. Hell, she'd take a week. She couldn't bear to stay here alone through the holidays.

For the next ten minutes, she tossed things into a suitcase without any plan or sense of order. Now that the decision was made, she only wanted to move quickly. She closed the lid on the suitcase, carried it into the living room and started for her coat.

The knock on her door had her clenching her teeth. If one more well-meaning neighbor stopped by to wish her Merry Christmas and invite her to dinner, she was going to scream.

She opened the door and felt the fresh wound stab through her. "Well, Macauley... Out wishing your tenants happy holidays?"

"Can I come in?"

"Why?"

"Nell." There was a wealth of patience in the word. "Please, let me come in."

"Fine, you own the place." She turned her back on him. "Sorry, I haven't any wassail, and I'm very low on good cheer."

"I need to talk to you." He'd been trying to find the right way and the right words for days.

"Really? Excuse me if I don't welcome it. The last time you needed to talk to me is still firmly etched in my mind."

"I didn't mean to make you cry."

"I cry easily. You should see me after a greeting-card commercial on TV." She couldn't keep up the snide comments, and she gave in, asking the question that was uppermost in her mind. "How are the kids?"

"Barely speaking to me." At her blank look, he gestured toward the couch. "Will you sit down? This is kind of a complicated story."

"I'll stand. I don't have a lot of time, actually. I was just leaving."

His gaze followed hers and landed on the suitcase. His mouth tightened. "Well, it didn't take long."

"What didn't?"

"I guess you took them up on that offer to teach back in New York."

"Word does travel. No, I didn't take them up. I like my job here, I like the people here, and I intend to stay. I'm just going on a holiday."

"You're going on a holiday at five o'clock on Christmas Eve?"

"I can come and go as I please. No, don't take off your coat," she snapped. Tears were threatening. "Just say your piece and get out. I still pay the rent here. On second thought, just leave now. Damn it, you're not going to make me cry again."

"The boys think Santa sent you."

"Excuse me?"

As the first tear spilled over, he moved to her, brushed it away with his thumb. "Don't cry, Nell. I hate knowing I made you cry."

"Don't touch me." She whirled away and fumbled a tissue out of the box.

He was discovering exactly how it felt to be sliced in two. "I'm sorry." Slowly he lowered his hand to his side. "I know how you must feel about me now."

"You don't know the half of it." She blew her nose, struggled for control. "What's this about the boys and Santa?"

"They wrote a letter back in the fall, not

long before they met you. They decided they wanted a mom for Christmas. Not *a* mom," Mac explained as she turned back to stare at him. "*The* mom. They keep correcting me on that one. They had pretty specific ideas about what they wanted. She was supposed to have yellow hair and smile a lot, like kids and dogs and bake cookies. They wanted bikes, too, but that was sort of an afterthought. All they really wanted was the mom."

"Oh." She did sit now, lowering herself onto the arm of the sofa. "That explains a couple of things." Steadying herself, she looked back at him. "Put you in quite a spot, didn't it? I know you love them, Mac, but starting a relationship with me to try to please your children takes things beyond parental devotion."

"I didn't know. Damn it, do you think I'd play with their feelings, or yours, that way?"

"Not theirs," she said hollowly. "Certainly not theirs."

He remembered how delicate she had seemed when they made love. There was more fragility now. No roses in her cheeks, he saw with a pang of distress. No light in her eyes. "I know what it's like to be hurt, Nell. I never would have hurt you deliberately. They didn't tell me about the letter until the night... You weren't the only one I made cry that night. I tried to explain that Santa doesn't work that way, but they've got it fixed in their heads that he sent you."

"I'll talk to them if you want me to."

"I don't deserve—"

"Not for you," she said. "For them."

He nodded, accepting. "I wondered how it would make you feel to know they wished for you."

"Don't push me, Mac."

He couldn't help it, and he kept his eyes on hers as he moved closer. "They wished for you for me, too. That's why they didn't tell me. You were our Christmas present." He reached down, touched her hair. "How does that make you feel?"

"How do you think I feel?" She batted his hand away and rose to face the window. "It hurts. I fell in love with the three of you almost from the first glance, and it hurts. Go away, leave me alone."

Somehow a fist had crept into his chest and was squeezing at his heart. "I thought you'd go away. I thought you'd leave us alone. I wouldn't let myself believe you cared enough to stay."

"Then you were an idiot," she mumbled.

"I was clumsy." He watched the tiny lights on her tree shining in her hair and gave up any thought of saving himself. "All right, I was an idiot. The worst kind, because I kept hiding from what you might feel, from what I felt. I didn't fall in love with you right away. At least I didn't know it. Not until the night of the concert. I wanted to tell you. I didn't know how to tell you. Then I heard something about the New York offer and it was the perfect excuse to push you out. I thought I was protecting the kids from getting hurt." No, he wouldn't use them, he thought in disgust. Not even to get her back. "That was only part of it. I was protecting myself. I couldn't control the way I felt about you. It scared me."

"Now's no different from then, Mac."

"It could be different." He took a chance and laid his hands on her shoulders, turned her to face him. "It took my own sons to show me that sometimes you've just got to wish. Don't leave me, Nell. Don't leave us."

"I was never going anywhere."

"Forgive me." She started to turn her head away, but he cupped her cheek, held it gently. "Please. Maybe I can't fix this, but give me a chance to try. I need you in my life. We need you."

There was such patience in his voice, such quiet strength in the hand on her face. Even as she looked at him, her heart began to heal. "I love you. All of you. I can't help it."

Relief and gratitude flavored the kiss as he touched his lips to hers. "I love you. I don't want to help it." Drawing her close, he cradled her head on his shoulder. "It's just been the three of us for so long, I didn't know how to make room. I think I'm figuring it out." He eased her away again and reached into his coat pocket. "I bought you a present."

"Mac." Still staggered from the roller-coaster emotions, she rubbed her hands over her damp cheeks. "It isn't Christmas yet."

"Close enough. I think if you'd open it now, I'd stop having all this tightness in my chest."

"All right." She dashed another tear aside. "We'll consider it a peace offering, then. I may even decide to…" She trailed off when the box was open in her hand. A ring, the traditional single diamond crowning a gold band.

"Marry me, Nell," he said quietly. "Be the mom."

She raised dazzled eyes to his. "You move awfully quickly for someone who always seems to take his time."

"Christmas Eve." He watched her face as he took the ring out of the box. "It seemed like the night to push my luck."

"It was a good choice." Smiling, she held out her hand. "A very good choice." When the ring was on her finger, she lifted her hand to his cheek. "When?"

He should have known it would be simple. With her, it would always be simple. "New Year's Eve's only a week away. It would be a good start to a new year. A new life."

"Yes."

"Will you come home with me tonight? I left the kids at Mira's. We could pick them up, and you'd spend Christmas where you belong." Before she could answer, he smiled and kissed her hand. "You're already packed."

"So I am. It must be magic."

"I'm beginning to believe it." He framed her face with his hands, lowered his mouth for a long, lingering kiss. "Maybe I didn't wish for you, but you're all I want for Christmas, Nell."

He rubbed his cheek over her hair, looked out at the colored lights gleaming on the houses below. "Did you hear something?" he murmured.

"Mmm..." She held him close, smiled. "Sleigh bells."

*   *   *   *   *

BL/33/TC

From No. 1 *New York Times* bestselling author Nora Roberts

Atop the rocky coast of Maine sits the Towers, a magnificent family mansion that is home to a legend of long-lost love, hidden emeralds— and four determined sisters.

Catherine, Amanda & Lilah
Featuring *Courting Catherine*, *A Man for Amanda* and *For the Love of Lilah*

Suzanna & Megan
Featuring *Suzanna's Surrender* and *Megan's Mate*

www.silhouette.co.uk

BL/34/TM

From No. 1 *New York Times* bestselling author Nora Roberts

The irresistible MacKade brothers are back and once again stirring the heart of every female that crosses their path.

Rafe and Jared
Featuring *The Return of Rafe MacKade* and
The Pride of Jared MacKade

Devin and Shane
Featuring *The Heart of Devin MacKade* and
The Fall of Shane MacKade

www.silhouette.co.uk

1106/XMAS TITLES a V2

All you could want for Christmas!

Meet handsome and seductive men under the mistletoe, escape to the world of Regency romance or simply relax by the fire with a heartwarming tale by one of our bestselling authors. These special stories will fill your holiday with Christmas sparkle!

On sale 6th October 2006

On sale 20th October 2006

1106/XMAS TITLES b V2

*On sale
3rd November
2006*

On sale 17th November 2006

*On sale
1st December
2006*

*Available at
WHSmith, Asda,
Tesco and all
good bookshops*

www.millsandboon.co.uk

M&B

1206/102/MB063 V2

Two families needed a little Christmas magic...

The Christmas Cradle by Linda Warren

As a surprise man enters Marisa Preston's life again,
she has to decide, does she really want to be a
mother to his child?

Daddy by Christmas by Mollie Molay

Strangers and the single parents to twins: does a
mix up at the fertility clinic mean that they have
to get married?

On sale 17th November 2006

www.millsandboon.co.uk

1206/055/MB066 V2

Unwrap three gorgeous men this holiday season!

For three women, the Christmas holidays bring more than just festive cheer – even as they try to escape the holiday celebrations and forget about absent partners or failed relationships.

What they don't realise is that you can't escape love, especially at Christmas time…

On sale 17th November 2006

www.millsandboon.co.uk

1106/082/MB060 V2

There's always something special about a new Christmas story from Debbie Macomber!

Being stuck in a plane with pilot Oliver Hamilton
during the festive season is not journalist
Emma Collins' idea of fun.

But as time draws on it seems Oliver is not quite
the Scrooge he appears…maybe there really *is*
something special about Christmas!

On sale 3rd November 2006

www.millsandboon.co.uk

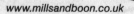